Dr. Nick Jameson

Colleen had known he would be at the wedding. Did he recognize her? She doubted it. How could he recognize someone he had never noticed before?

He saw her *now,* staring at her so intently that goose bumps rose on the bare skin of her shoulders and arms.

"Hi," he said. "I missed the rehearsal. Any idea which bridesmaid I walk down the aisle?"

She blinked her eyes open and met his gaze. In his expression there was a flirtatious twinkle. All rational thought fled her mind.

Probably used to women's tongue-tied reactions, he grinned, and a deep dimple pierced one lean cheek. "I'm the best man."

"Then you'll walk down the aisle with the maid of honor," she informed him. The haughty tone of her voice surprised her.

"I hope that's you," he said, flashing the dimpled grin at her.

Dear Reader,

Welcome back to Cloverville, Michigan, for the second book in my THE WEDDING PARTY series for Harlequin American Romance. Even if you didn't read *Unexpected Bride*, you'll have no problem figuring out what's going on now in the small town of Cloverville, because all four books in the series cover the same time frame. Since the stories occur simultaneously, you may recognize some scenes from *Unexpected Bride*, but from the interesting new perspectives of the best man, Dr. Nick Jameson, and bridesmaid and younger sister of the bride, Colleen McClintock.

Colleen has had a crush on Dr. Jameson forever, but Nick first notices Colleen at the wedding of her sister to his best friend. These two commitment-phobes have no intention of taking a trek down the aisle themselves. But Nick brings out the impulsive nature Colleen has long suppressed, and Colleen turns Nick's world upside down. I hope you enjoy reading their story!

Happy reading!

Lisa Childs

The Best Man's Bride
LISA CHILDS

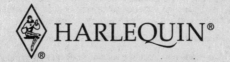

HARLEQUIN®

TORONTO • NEW YORK • LONDON
AMSTERDAM • PARIS • SYDNEY • HAMBURG
STOCKHOLM • ATHENS • TOKYO • MILAN • MADRID
PRAGUE • WARSAW • BUDAPEST • AUCKLAND

ISBN-13: 978-0-373-75214-0
ISBN-10:   0-373-75214-8

THE BEST MAN'S BRIDE

ABOUT THE AUTHOR

Bestselling, award-winning author Lisa Childs writes paranormal and contemporary romance for Harlequin/Silhouette Books. She lives on thirty acres in west Michigan with her husband, two daughters, a talkative Siamese and a long-haired Chihuahua who thinks she's a rottweiler. Lisa loves hearing from readers, who can contact her through her Web site, www.lisachilds.com, or snail mail address, P.O. Box 139, Marne, MI 49435.

Books by Lisa Childs

HARLEQUIN AMERICAN ROMANCE
1198—UNEXPECTED BRIDE

HARLEQUIN NEXT
TAKING BACK MARY ELLEN BLACK
LEARNING TO HULA
CHRISTMAS PRESENCE
  "Secret Santa"

HARLEQUIN INTRIGUE
664—RETURN OF THE LAWMAN
720—SARAH'S SECRETS
758—BRIDAL RECONNAISSANCE
834—THE SUBSTITUTE SISTER

For my wonderful, supportive, talented friends:
Mary Gardner and Kimberly Duffy,
finalists in the Romance Writers of America 2007
Golden Heart writing contest—
ladies, you're both winners with me!

Acknowledgments:

With great appreciation to Kathleen Scheibling
and my agent, Jenny Bent, for offering their
guidance and sharing their knowledge.

Chapter One

"Are you sure you know what you're doing?" Nick Jameson asked his best friend.

"I was going to ask *you* that," Josh Towers said as he peered into the mirror on the wall of the groom's dressing room, straightening a bow tie that was already perfectly straight. But then, nearly everything about Josh was perfect—apart from his taste in women.

Nick sighed. "What do *I* need to know? I'm not getting married." *Not ever.*

"You missed the rehearsal, you know."

"Hey, I was on call last night." Nick shrugged, testing the seams on his tuxedo jacket. Tuxedos were called monkey suits for a reason, he thought. They were damned near as comfortable as straitjackets.

Not that he'd ever been in a straitjacket, but if for some reason he considered doing what Josh was—getting married— he'd put himself in one.

"And what's so hard about what I have to do?" Nick asked his friend. He had stood up with Josh at his other wedding— the first one. He was such a hypocrite. How could he stand up for something in which he put no faith? "I just walk down the aisle with some girl on my arm."

"You're the best man," Josh reminded him. "You're in charge of the rings, too." He dug a pair of gold bands out of his pocket and handed them over.

The metal, although warm from Josh's pocket, chilled Nick's skin as the rings lay in his palm. The anxiety built in his throat, nearly choking him. He didn't even like to touch the things.

"Daddy," one of Josh's twin four-year-old sons said, "we're the ring bears."

"Funny, you don't look like bears," Nick teased, chucking the boy under the chin. Must have been Buzz since his black hair had been kept *buzzed* short for the past two years after he'd gotten hold of Josh's electric razor. TJ's hair was a little longer and moussed into half-inch spikes. Both twins had deep blue eyes, and now they stared up at him as if he were trying to make off with one of their Tonka trucks.

"Yeah," said TJ as he tugged on Nick's pant leg. The twins' tuxedos matched his, black with white pleated shirts, black bow ties and red cummerbunds. "We're supposed to carry the rings."

Nick would gladly have handed over the gold bands, but he doubted Josh would trust them to the devilish duo. The boys had a well-known penchant for "flushing" things, including their dad's pager and cell phone.

"Hey, buddy," Nick said to his best friend, "I'll let you handle this one." With a grin, he ducked out of the groom's room, leaving Josh alone with his unruly twin sons.

No wonder the guy had decided to marry a woman he barely knew. The boys had him outnumbered and he needed help fast—he needed a mother for his sons. Although Nick understood Josh's reasons, he didn't agree with his friend's decision. After the boys' mom had taken off when the twins were just babies, why would Josh *ever* trust another woman?

Nick would never make that mistake, not that he didn't think some women were worthy of trust. His dad swore his mother had been a paragon of virtue. Nick, himself, had never known her. He'd been younger than the twins when she died. It wasn't that he mistrusted *all* women, so much as that he really didn't trust himself. If a guy as smart as Josh hadn't had the sense to fall for the right woman, a guy like Nick didn't stand a chance.

Hearing the outraged howl that signaled a major temper tantrum in the groom's room, Nick walked farther away from the door. Sure, he could have gone inside and tried to help out—he was the best man, after all. But Nick was going to have the boys all to himself during Josh's honeymoon. If he hadn't already sworn off marriage and fatherhood, he was damned sure he would after two weeks with the twins.

Another door opened farther down the hall and a group of women spilled out. A young girl dressed like a miniature bride, a blonde, a redhead and a brunette, all dressed in shiny red strapless gowns. Which one of them was he supposed to walk down the aisle?

Maybe he *should* have come to the rehearsal, but Cloverville, Michigan, was more than an hour from where he worked in Grand Rapids. He sighed. Now he wouldn't be working only in Grand Rapids; he and Josh would have a practice in Cloverville as soon as their new offices were finished. Personally, he hoped the contractors took their damn sweet time. If Josh wasn't his best friend, Nick wouldn't have let the other man talk him into opening their office here. He had no interest in Cloverville.

Then the brunette turned, her rich brown hair moving like a silk curtain around her bare shoulders. His fingers itched with the need to touch it, to see if her hair could possibly be as soft as those chocolate-colored strands appeared. Her gaze met his then, and he realized that her eyes were as deep a brown as her hair.

Nick's chest clenched and his breath caught, as if he'd slammed on the brakes and his seat belt had pulled too tight. Heat flushed his face and dampened his palms. So that he wouldn't lose the rings before the ceremony, he wrapped his fingers tightly around them and shoved them deep into his pocket. Even his hand shook. What the hell had just happened to him?

DR. NICK JAMESON. Colleen McClintock had known, of course, that he would be at the wedding. He was, after all, the best man. Did he recognize her? Colleen doubted it. How could he recognize someone he had never even noticed before?

And yet he saw her *now,* staring at her so intently that goose bumps rose on the bare skin of her shoulders and arms. She regretted talking Brenna out of matching wraps—the maid of honor had been right. Colleen should have risked fumbling the flowers or tripping on the shawl for a little more cover-up.

But between her bad luck and her innate clumsiness, she hadn't wanted to risk embarrassing herself or her sister. That was probably why Molly had chosen her longtime friend Brenna Kelly as maid of honor instead of Colleen. She'd worried that her little sister would mess up her important day. Or maybe she'd never considered Colleen at all. Kind of like Dr. Nick Jameson hadn't noticed she existed until today.

Was it the red dress Brenna had chosen? The strapless sheath of satin had somehow produced curves Colleen hadn't been aware she possessed. And the color was so vibrant—for the first time in a long while she didn't feel invisible.

"We need to get lined up," Brenna ordered the others. The wedding party immediately responded to her command. Even

Colleen's headstrong teenage brother, Rory, who never paid attention to anyone, now meekly joined the group outside the bride's dressing room. Maybe that was why Molly had chosen the redhead as maid of honor. People listened to Brenna Kelly, whereas they rarely heard Colleen.

Of course that was her fault. She'd always been quiet so that her older sister and her friends wouldn't notice her tagging along. But Molly had never made her feel unwelcome, and over the years her friends had become Colleen's, as well. Brenna Kelly with her gorgeous red hair and generous curves, and Abby Hamilton, the petite, vivacious blonde, were the best friends Colleen had ever known. Eric South, the lone male member of their group of friends, had backed out of the wedding party just before the rehearsal dinner the previous evening.

So Colleen's older brother, Clayton, had been left with an additional responsibility. As well as filling in for their dad, who'd died eight years ago, and giving away the bride, he also had to walk Abby down the aisle in Eric's place. Clayton probably would have preferred walking Abby out the door. He'd always blamed her, unjustly, for any trouble his sisters had gotten into. He had already pulled Abby aside for a private conversation, no doubt warning her not to start anything.

But Colleen hoped that Abby would start something—with Clayton. He needed someone like Abby to loosen him up, to teach him how to play. He'd had to grow up far too fast when their father died—they'd all had to grow up. But Abby, who'd lived away from Cloverville for the past eight years, swore she and her daughter had only come home for the wedding. Abby edged closer to the rest of the wedding party, but early guests had gathered around her and her four-year-old daughter, the miniature bride, clad in a gorgeous white dress.

What about Molly? Had she managed to get into her

wedding gown? She'd shooed everyone out of the dressing room before anyone could help her. Colleen turned back toward the closed door. Nerves fluttered in her stomach. Poor Molly.

Even though she hadn't admitted it out loud, Molly clearly had been having doubts about getting married. Despite being three years younger, Colleen was close to her sister. Actually, Molly had always been more friend than sister. She'd never resented Colleen shadowing her. Why now, when Molly should have been leaning on her friends for support, had she begged them to leave her all alone?

"Hello," a deep voice murmured, pulling Colleen's attention back to him.

Dr. Nick Jameson had crossed the hall and now stood in front of her. Even in heels she had to tip her head back a bit to focus on his face and stop thinking about how his broad shoulders filled out his black tux. While he looked handsome enough in scrubs, he was completely devastating in a tuxedo. Sun streaked through the church doors at the end of the hall and glinted off his golden-blond hair so that Colleen had to close her eyes for a moment.

Dizziness rushed over her, but instead of seeing spots behind her closed lids she saw his face, his pale green eyes staring down at her.

"Hi," he said, his voice a bit hoarse. "I missed the rehearsal. Any idea which bridesmaid I walk down the aisle?"

Colleen blinked her eyes open again and met his gaze. In his eyes there was a flirtatious twinkle. All rational thought fled her mind.

Probably used to women's tongue-tied reactions, he grinned, and a deep dimple pierced one lean cheek. "I'm the best man."

He said it as if he was claiming more than his title in the wedding party. Although his arrogance came as no surprise, Colleen lifted a brow.

"Then you'll walk down the aisle with the maid of honor," she said. The haughty tone of her own voice surprised her, and she swallowed a shocked gasp. Usually she spoke so soft and quietly that people asked her to repeat herself, if they even realized she'd said something in the first place.

"I hope that's you," he said, flashing the dimpled grin at her.

The volunteers and nurses at the hospital in Grand Rapids—where Nick was on staff and Colleen volunteered— would have been envious of Colleen receiving one of "Dr. Yummy's" rare grins. Her knees, and other parts of her, quivered in reaction. But when she opened her mouth, the haughty voice said, "No, I'm not the maid of honor."

He pressed a hand against his heart as if she'd hurt him, but then he flashed the grin again and teased, "So you're not a maid of *honor?*"

Honor? An honorable person wouldn't have let a friend take the blame for something she'd done, no matter what the circumstances. While Colleen fumbled for a response to his flirty question, Brenna bustled up.

"Places, everyone," she barked.

NICK KICKED HIMSELF FOR whatever he'd said that had drained all the color from the brunette's face and left her eyes dark, wide and haunted. She was so young, probably only in her early twenties. What could she possibly know of dishonor?

"You're Dr. Jameson," said the redheaded bridesmaid who'd just joined them. She didn't even give him a chance to respond before nudging him toward the front of the line.

"We can switch, if he wants," muttered the teenage boy Nick had met briefly before the kid, Rory McClintock, had skipped outside for air. The curly-haired kid took Nick's place at the brunette's side. "It's lame to walk my *sister* down the aisle."

The boy was the bride's brother, Nick knew. So the brown-haired bridesmaid must be her younger sister. All the McClintocks had the same basic coloring—dark hair, dark eyes. Nick could barely remember the bride's name, let alone the names of all of her relatives. Of course Josh hadn't known the girl, Mandy…Mindy… Molly—that was it. Josh hadn't known Molly very long before he'd proposed. Not nearly long enough to decide to spend the rest of his life with her. But then, given Josh's history, maybe he'd resigned himself to take however long he could get.

Nick shook his head. He'd rather live alone than trust someone to love him forever. But Josh didn't have the option of living alone—he had twin boys to raise. Buzz and TJ exploded into the hallway in a tangle of arms, legs and raised voices. With one word from the redhead, however, they fell into line.

As the first notes of the wedding march pealed out, the maid of honor grabbed Nick's arm and started down the aisle. Nick quickened his pace, to keep from being dragged. He glanced toward her and saw that no smile brightened her face or eyes. Her attitude matched his. *Let's get this over with.*

In a minute they'd reached the altar and she released his arm. Before stepping to the bride's side, she stopped in front of Josh, who was waiting next to the minister. She drew an audible, shaky breath and then moved aside as Nick took his position behind Josh.

Since they'd been kids, they'd watched each other's backs: teaming up to conquer playground bullies in elementary school, studying together to pass physics in college, then supporting each other through med school. Now, in their venture into private practice, they remained best friends. Nick patted Josh's shoulder, which was tense beneath his palm. Maybe he'd finally realized what a mistake he was making.

"You can stop this," Nick murmured, under the swell of organ music.

Josh's head swiveled toward him. He'd heard Nick's comment and from his glare he didn't think much of it. Of course Josh was too nice a guy to back out at the altar and humiliate the bride. The groom turned to face the aisle and so did Nick.

The older brother of the bride, whom Nick had also met in the groom's room, walked toward them with the blonde. When he left her, almost reluctantly, at the altar, he walked past Josh and then Nick before continuing around the side of the pews and heading for the back. To get the bride. Josh had explained that the bride's dad had died eight years ago. So apparently Clayton McClintock pulled double duty as a groomsman and stand-in for father of the bride.

Nick turned and focused on the brunette who walked down the aisle now, holding her younger brother's arm. She wouldn't have been that old when her dad died, probably not much older than her teenage brother was now. Nick winced in commiseration—not over his mother, whom he really didn't remember. He'd lost someone else close to him when he'd been a teenager, however. If not for Josh and his friendship, Nick probably wouldn't have survived that dark period. He owed Josh, and opening an office in Cloverville was small repayment.

Who had *she* had to lean on when her dad died—her family, friends? Was she like him, in that she had never completely recovered from her loss? Maybe that was why, despite her haughty tone, he'd picked up on vulnerability—even a fragility—in her expressive eyes and delicate face.

The sunshine streaming through the stained-glass windows highlighted the deep brown of her shimmering hair. His heart shifted, pressing against his ribs. Damn, she was beautiful.

What was her name? Had he ever heard it? Probably. But he hadn't cared. *Then.*

Now he cared too much. As she released her brother's arm, she peered briefly at Nick through her thick black lashes. Blood rushed through his veins, and he felt light-headed.

No, he didn't care. He just hadn't had enough sleep or food in the past week—damn crazy shifts at the hospital. Maybe Josh was right; maybe the lighter hours of a private practice would be better for them both. Opening their own office wasn't a new idea. They'd planned it since medical school. But Nick hadn't thought they'd make the move quite so soon.

The twins headed down the aisle next, having a tug-of-war over the ring bearer's pillow; once white, it was now smudged with small, chocolate fingerprints. Josh needed more time with his kids. But what would Nick do with extra free time besides sleep? With an effort, he kept his focus on the aisle, refusing to give in to the urge to glance across the altar at the lissome brunette.

Behind the boys, the flower girl walked at a much slower pace, carefully dropping red rose petals onto the white runner. Laughter at her diligence rippled over the wedding guests like the wave at a football game. The organ music intensified dramatically. Nick shuddered at what he'd always considered the ominous tone of the wedding march. The guests rose and turned toward the back of the church.

Nick sure hoped he was wrong about Josh rushing to the altar. He wished a long, happy marriage for his best friend with a woman who would *always* love him and his sons. He hoped Molly McClintock was that woman.

Like the guests, Nick turned toward the bride's entrance. But the only person he saw was Clayton McClintock, standing alone on the rose-strewn white runner.

Where the hell is the bride? The thought chased through Nick's mind as the organ music halted abruptly. Shocked murmurs rose from the guests, quieting to hushed whispers.

Offering reassurance, Nick grabbed Josh's shoulder, which wasn't nearly as tense as it had been moments ago. "God, man, I'm sorry," he murmured, his voice hoarse with emotion. He couldn't imagine the emotions pummeling Josh but worried over the toll they'd take on his friend.

Nick glanced toward the other side of the altar, toward the bride's sister. Despite his attraction to her, he would never put himself in Josh's vulnerable position. He would never be anyone's groom.

"The wedding is going to be slightly delayed," Clayton said. "The bride is not quite ready yet, so we appreciate your patience. Thank you."

Nick snorted, recognizing a load of bull when he heard it. Apparently, the blond bridesmaid thought so, too, as she took off at a run toward the back of the church. Clayton McClintock caught her, slowing her down, and the music began—again. The twins, probably thinking a game of tag was afoot, chased each other down the aisle.

The young flower girl, much better behaved than the twins, took the arm of the teenage boy who'd accompanied his sister, leaving the brunette to walk alone as the rest of the wedding party filed out. Nick fell into step beside her, his shoulder nearly brushing hers as they shared the narrow white runner. Sunlight painted her bare skin gold. His fingers ached to touch, to caress her delicate shoulders and arms. To be a proper escort, he crooked his elbow, extending his forearm to her.

She hesitated a moment before extending her hand. Her fingers clutched the sleeve of his jacket, the warmth of her touch penetrating the material. Nick tensed, his body reacting to her closeness. His lungs hurt from the pressure of holding his breath. He'd never been so instantly attracted to a woman. Why her? They'd barely spoken to each other. He didn't even know her name.

And how could he think about anything but what Josh was going through? He was a terrible friend. He pulled his attention away from the bridesmaid to glance back over his shoulder. *Poor Josh.*

The redheaded maid of honor had the groom now, clutching his arm and just about dragging him down the aisle as she had Nick. Except now it was over and done with. No matter what the bride's brother had told the guests, Nick doubted the wedding was just delayed.

What a mess. Anger surged, heating his blood. How dare the bride change her mind now and humiliate such a fine man. Despite Nick being the best man, Josh was the *better* man. He always treated people with kindness and respect. He didn't deserve to be hurt like this. Again.

Just like Josh's first wife, Molly McClintock had sought him out while she was volunteering at the hospital. *Yeah, right.* Setting a mantrap. That's what she'd done. And she'd caught him, manipulating him into a marriage proposal after just a few short months of dating. She'd accepted Josh's proposal and taken his ring. Then she'd stood him up? Her betrayal proved what Nick had known for a long time. *Women were not to be trusted.*

Sure, there were *some* honest ones—like his mother, for example—but how was a man to know which ones were after his heart and which ones his wallet?

Chapter Two

Colleen matched her steps to Nick's as they walked down the aisle and crossed the hall with the rest of the wedding party except for Clayton and Abby, who already stood inside the bride's dressing room, nose to nose, as they argued.

Of course Clayton would blame Abby. And of course he'd be furious. Feeling responsible, as always, for all his father's duties, Clayton had taken it upon himself to pay for the wedding and give away the bride. He'd said he couldn't wait to have one less responsibility. Poor Clayton.

He just didn't get it. He actually loved being in charge of his younger siblings. Colleen worked for him at the insurance agency he'd taken over after their father died. Although Clayton had given her the title of office manager, he'd never really given her any responsibility. So she didn't feel all that guilty for the two afternoons a week she spent volunteering at the hospital in Grand Rapids, where the best man and the groom were on staff.

The jilted groom.

The wedding dress hung from a hook on one of the white walls, almost blending in but for the lace and satin that stirred in the breeze blowing through the open window. Molly had run away? Colleen's stomach churned. Molly was too smart and strong to run. When they were growing up, Colleen had been the one to constantly run away—although no one had ever noticed. So she'd always come home, and Molly would, too. Safe and sound. She had to.

Abby's argument with Clayton subsided as she unfolded a crumpled note. Of course Molly would have left a note. She'd always been as responsible as their older brother.

"What does it say?" Clayton demanded, asking the question that was burning on everyone else's lips. "Come on, I'm worried about her. I want to know what it says!"

"It's a good thing that she ran off," Abby said, "before making the biggest mistake of her life."

The groom gasped in surprise, and the muscles in Nick's left arm tightened beneath Colleen's fingers. His pale green eyes darkened with anger and a muscle twitched in his jaw, as if he had clenched his teeth to hold in something he was dying to say.

"Josh, I'm sorry." Clayton offered the apology first, used to assuming responsibility for everyone else. Even Abby?

Nick's tension didn't ease, not even when the kids chattered, the twins pulling petals off each other's boutonnieres. Colleen pulled her hand from his arm and curled her fingers into her palm to quell the tingling. She should have let go of him long ago. Actually she never should have touched him in the first place. He'd made no secret of his disdain for long-term relationships; the other volunteers and the hospital staff had warned her not to develop a crush on the handsome doctor. Nothing would come of it but a broken heart.

"I'm sorry." Abby offered her apology to Josh. "She doesn't say that in the note…about making a mistake. She's just really confused right now."

"What's going on?" Rory asked, tugging loose the knot of his bow tie. Colleen was surprised her kid brother had kept it tied as long as he had. "Did Molly really skip out?"

Clayton shrugged. "Ask Abby. She's the one with the explanation."

"Is she all right?" Josh asked. His handsome face held none of the anger that was darkening his friend's eyes.

From her years of volunteering at the hospital, Colleen felt she knew him well. Unlike Dr. Jameson Josh *had* noticed her, although not the way he'd noticed her sister, who'd only volunteered when she'd had time around her med school classes and studying. Even if he and Molly hadn't dated all that long, Colleen understood why her big sister had accepted his proposal. Besides being ridiculously handsome, with dark hair and bright blue eyes, Dr. Joshua Towers was a genuinely nice guy.

"She's okay," Abby assured him as she clutched the note.

Colleen wasn't surprised that Molly had trusted Abby with her explanation. She could keep a secret and she would only share what Molly wanted everyone to know.

Abby continued, "She's just confused right now. She needs some time alone to figure out what she really wants."

"Maybe she should have figured *that* out before she accepted Josh's proposal. It's pretty damned flaky to back out at the altar," Nick muttered, pushing his hand through his hair and squeezing the back of his neck.

"Molly is not flaky!" How dare he say anything like that about her sister? He didn't even know her. Neither had the groom, sadly. Despite dating for a few months, Molly had admitted that due to their crazy schedules, she and Josh hadn't gone on that many dates. Was that why Molly had backed out of the wedding?

Actually, why had Molly, the focused and sensible McClintock sister, agreed to marry a virtual *stranger?* Even if he was nice and handsome. Molly wasn't the type to believe in love at first sight. *She* never acted impetuously.

Colleen had always been the impetuous one. If any McClintock were to fall in love at first sight, *she* would be the foolish one.

"It's my fault," Josh said, with a heavy sigh. "I rushed her into this, even though I knew she wasn't ready."

Nick gripped his friend's shoulder. "Don't blame yourself. She could have told you no. This just goes to show you, *they* can't be trusted."

Colleen sucked in a breath, but she couldn't really argue. She'd told lies. She'd kept secrets. Nick Jameson was wrong about her sister, but right about her. *She* couldn't be trusted, despite how careful she'd been the past eight years to always do the right thing. She couldn't trust herself not to do something foolish again. Like fall for a man who didn't believe in love…

FAIRY LIGHTS IN RED and white cast a romantic pink glow, disguising the worn linoleum and painted paneling of the American Legion Hall, which everyone in Cloverville used for their wedding receptions. The biggest facility in town, the hall also hosted anniversary parties, graduation open houses and funeral luncheons.

Funereal described the mood of the wedding party, or at least Colleen's mood as she stood before the gift table. Her eyes misted and all the vivid colors of the wrapping paper swirled into a kaleidoscope. Molly had asked for time alone to sort things out. But selfishly Colleen wanted to see her sister, to talk to her, so that *she* could sort things out, too. Like her feelings for a certain blond doctor. His noticing her, finally, had intensified those emotions, so that they couldn't be dismissed like a harmless crush anymore. And as Colleen had learned in high school, there really wasn't anything harmless about a crush.

An arm slid around Colleen's waist and she received a gentle hug. She turned toward her mother. "We should have canceled the reception," she told Mary McClintock.

Yet Colleen understood her mother's reasoning in insisting they not cancel. Cloverville's only caterer, Mrs. George, who was the sole provider for her family, had been cooking for days. She'd had help from Brenna's parents, the Kellys, too. Regret filled Colleen at the thought of all their hard work going to waste. In addition, her mother had pointed out, the whole town had been looking forward to a party.

"And let all that food go to waste?" Her mother tsked, then shook her head, tumbling soft brown curls around her face. "Your brother would have a fit, since he paid for it."

Colleen's lips twitched into a reluctant smile. "He's probably having a fit about paying for it now." Since their mother, the minute everyone had arrived at the hall, had turned the reception into a welcome home party for Abby Hamilton, the girl Clayton had always considered a bad influence on his sisters. Her smile slid away as guilt took hold. If he only knew that the real troublemaker had been his little sister.

Mom's arm wound tighter around her waist. *Did her mother know?* Over the years Colleen sometimes had suspected that she did.

"Ah, it's good for your brother when everything doesn't go exactly according to his plan." Once he'd realized there would be repercussions if he canceled the reception, he'd planned to turn it into an open house for the town. But his mother had had other plans. "*Abby* would be good for your brother."

A smile pulled at Colleen's lips. "Subtle, Mom."

"You disagree?"

Colleen shook her head. "No." Her older brother had always fascinated and infuriated Abby Hamilton and the reverse was equally true. "But throwing a welcome-home party for Abby doesn't guarantee she's actually going to move home."

She sighed, thinking of the night before and their impromptu slumber party/bachelorette party, during which she'd tried to convince Abby to come home for good. Abby was looking for a location for the next franchise of her employment agency, Temps to Go. Colleen's argument that Cloverville, which was growing rapidly, would be the perfect location had fallen on deaf ears. "In fact, she's pretty set against moving back."

Mary McClintock's smile didn't slip, and her dark eyes twinkled. "Then we'll have to change her mind, won't we?"

"Okay." Colleen had learned long ago that it was easier to agree than argue with her mother. "I'm not going to play matchmaker with you, though." Probably Abby and Clayton were both too stubborn to ever admit to the attraction that had always simmered between them. "But I want Abby and Lara to move back to Cloverville."

And not just so Colleen wouldn't continue to feel so guilty over her leaving. She'd missed her friend. E-mails, phone calls and letters weren't adequate to fully convey the force of nature that was Abby Hamilton in person. *Poor Clayton…*

"I want Molly to come home, too," Colleen admitted. "I'm worried about her."

"Who says your sister isn't home?"

"I called the house," Colleen admitted. "No one answered. Do you think she just went home?"

Her mother shook her head. "She's not at our house."

"You know where she is?"

"I think we all know where she is."

With Eric. He had always been the friend to whom Molly had turned for comfort and support. Maybe she'd backed out of her wedding just because he hadn't been there.

"She's okay," her mother assured Colleen. "She just needs time, like she said in her note."

Colleen narrowed her eyes and studied her mother's carefully blank expression. "You talked to her," she accused. Colleen, as well as Abby and Brenna, had tried Molly's cell, but it had been turned off. They'd even tried Eric's, but he'd claimed Molly wasn't with him. But then, no one had ever been able to lie to Mary McClintock except Colleen.

"Look at all these gifts," her mother said, suddenly changing the subject, as she gestured at the crowded table. In addition to the gifts, cards overflowed from a wishing well that Colleen had constructed out of cardboard and wrapping paper.

"We'll have to send everything back."

"I'll have Clayton make an announcement for people to pick up their presents before they leave." Her mother sighed. "Or maybe *I* should do that. He has enough responsibility."

"Clayton thrives on responsibility." While he might grumble about paying for the reception, he would not allow anyone else to assume the duty he considered, like so many others, to be his. Dr. Towers had already said that he would pay for the reception, but Clayton had insisted.

Mary McClintock shook her head. "He needs more in life. He needs a wife. Children."

Colleen snorted, well aware of the fact that her brother shared Dr. Jameson's views on marriage. He had no intention of ever having a wedding of his own.

Her derision didn't faze her mom, however, who continued, "The same things you need."

"A wife?" she teased, used to dealing with her mother's not-so-subtle attempts at matchmaking. Mary McClintock refused to accept that Colleen wasn't ready for marriage—not now, and maybe not ever.

Mom squeezed her waist. "A husband."

An image of Dr. Nick Jameson, standing at the altar, flashed into her mind, and Colleen's pulse quickened. "I'm only twenty-three."

Her mother smiled wistfully. "I was barely twenty when I married your father."

And look how that had ended, with more heartache than any woman should have to endure.

Colleen blinked again to clear the mist from her eyes. That was why she wasn't ready. She wasn't strong enough yet to deal with the kind of loss her mother had experienced. She doubted she would ever be that strong. She far preferred unrequited crushes to a relationship.

"You and the best man made quite the dashing couple when he escorted you out of the church," her mother observed. "I wasn't the only one to notice."

Colleen bit the inside of her cheek, but the arrival of several of the town busybodies saved her from responding. The organist, Mrs. Hild, in a wildflower-patterned dress and wide-brimmed hat, pulled her mother into a hug. "Oh, Mary, you were so brave to turn the-wedding-that-wasn't into a party."

The wedding-that-wasn't.

"And generous," Mrs. Carpenter added. She was married to the owner of the hardware store, one of the thriftiest men in town.

"Poor Molly," Mrs. Hild murmured.

Poor Molly. They shouldn't be having her reception without her. Despite her request for time alone, they should probably be out looking for her. Maybe Eric had been telling the truth, and Molly really wasn't with him. Colleen knew how it felt to run away and have no one care enough to come looking. She murmured some excuse, letting her mother handle the gossips. As she walked away, Colleen passed the cake table. The five-tier confection rose in a pyramid to the little plastic figurine standing at the top. Alone. Just the groom. The bride was gone.

"THIS IS A MISTAKE," Nick said, letting the door close behind him as he stepped inside the men's restroom with the jilted groom.

Josh crossed the green tile floor to a row of old porcelain sinks, then ran water over his palms to splash on his face. "I'm surprised you've controlled yourself this long."

Nick tensed. "What?"

He should have known that he could hide nothing from his oldest, closest friend. Josh must have noticed how hard Nick had fought his attraction to the young bridesmaid, which hadn't been easy plastered against her in the back of a limousine. Trying to make some space between the two of them, he'd inadvertently knocked the maid of honor off the end of the bench seat. He had to focus on his friend now, and not on some female who would probably prove as untrustworthy as her sister.

"I don't know how you managed to wait this long to say I told you so." Josh's hands shook as he dragged them over his face.

"Man, that's not why…"

"You followed me into the bathroom?" Josh finished for him.

"We shouldn't even be here," Nick said. "This is a mistake, coming to your reception when you've skipped the wedding."

"*I* didn't skip the wedding." Josh laughed. "Only the bride skipped the wedding."

"Why are we here?" Nick asked, concern for his friend in-

creasing. Josh had had a rough time when his first wife abandoned him and the boys. What must he be going through
now? Besides the obvious denial?

"Like Mrs. McClintock said back at the church," Josh
reminded him, "the food is already paid for."

By the bride's brother. But Josh had tried to pay—Nick had
heard him offer more than once. That was the kind of guy Josh
was, generous and selfless. Nick shook his head, bemused as
always, that they were friends when they were so different.

"The whole town was looking forward to a party, and like
I reminded you in the limo," Josh continued, "we're opening
an office here. We need to meet our potential patients."

Nick didn't need the reminder about the office. Even before
the bride had vanished, he'd been against opening a practice
in Cloverville. While he couldn't argue that the town was
growing, it still wasn't big city enough for him or close
enough to the hospital where they had surgical privileges. But
Josh's dream had always been to open a small-town practice,
a partnership. Nick had made Josh's dream his—except for
the small-town part. "All two patients?" he scoffed.

Josh snorted. "We're going to have more than that. The
only other doctor in town retired last year."

"Retired or went bankrupt," Nick muttered. "And he was
a G.P. We're not general practitioners. Does this town really
need an orthopedic surgeon and a plastic surgeon?"

"Plastic surgery may be my specialty, but I intend to handle
more," Josh reminded him. "Cloverville's just in the burbs of
Grand Rapids. We still have surgical privileges at the hospital.
We'll have plenty of patients. They just have to get to know us."

Nick wasn't comfortable with anyone getting to know him.

"That's why we're *here,*" Josh continued.

"You didn't have to come," Nick pointed out. They hadn't

had to use the limo, either, even though it had already been paid for, too. But the entire wedding party had ridden together to the reception—well, everyone but the bride. "I could have represented us here."

"And ushered us into the poorhouse," Josh teased. "You'd scare away more patients than you'd attract. You're not exactly known for your bedside manner."

Who had time for small talk? He'd never had. He'd rather repair people's broken bones or replace their hips and knees than discuss the weather. "I'm a surgeon."

"I am, too."

Dr. Joshua Towers had a bedside manner other doctors envied. Everyone loved Josh. Well, everyone but the women he loved. How did someone so smart keep falling for unsuitable women? Not that Molly McClintock had *seemed* unsuitable. As well as being beautiful, she was smart. Nick personally knew how tough medical school was. And the few times Nick had met her, she'd seemed sweet—far sweeter than Josh's money-grubbing ex. In fact, she'd seemed the exact opposite of Amy. No wonder Josh had proposed so quickly.

"You're also a man who just got left at the altar," Nick said, knowing Josh was used to, and even relied on, his brutal honesty. When he needed it, Josh had always been there for him. "No one expected you to show up for the reception after what just happened. Come on, what's really going on with you?"

Josh offered a halfhearted smile. "The boys wanted to party."

Nick narrowed his eyes as his suspicions grew. "You think she'll show up here? Is that what you're doing? Waiting for *her?*"

Although he hadn't really gotten to know Molly McClintock,

he doubted she'd have the guts to show her face to the whole town after the stunt she'd just pulled. "She's not coming."

"Probably not," Josh agreed.

Probably. So he held out some hope. Just how optimistic could the guy be? Too damned optimistic, Nick answered his own question.

Josh sighed. "I'm staying in Cloverville, and I know I should have told you this already. I don't have possession of it yet, but I've bought a house here—for me and the boys."

And the woman he'd intended to marry. Nick's guts twisted with his friend's pain.

"Why'd you do that?" He scrubbed a hand through his hair, trying to hold both his temper and his tongue. "The office isn't going to be done for a while."

"But it *will* be done, Nick."

"Maybe it shouldn't be."

"We have a lot of money invested."

Nick massaged the tense cords that stood out on the back of his neck. "This is a bad idea."

Josh lifted his head, and Nick met his gaze in the mirror. "*You* can't back out on me."

"Never. You know that, man. I got your back." He sighed. "The practice isn't the bad idea. It's this *town* that is."

"You never wanted the office here," Josh conceded.

Nick resurrected his old argument. "It's too far from the hospital. We can't do surgeries out of the office…" If they got any business at all.

"But you agreed."

"Because you're my best friend." Agitated, Nick blew out a ragged sigh. "And you thought there was something here for you."

"There's still something here for me."

"She left you at the altar," Nick said even though he was sure the jilted groom didn't need the reminder. "Why would you still want her?"

Josh's blue eyes hardened with determination. "I want to *talk* to her."

"You're…"

"Crazy?"

He certainly hoped not. He didn't want his best friend doing anything stupid. Nick had already lost someone he loved to a broken heart—his older brother, Bruce, had fallen apart when his pregnant wife left him. Devastated to find out that the baby she was carrying wasn't his, he'd started to drink. And he hadn't stopped until he drove into a tree. Nick hadn't been able to save his big brother, from his pain or from himself.

But he wouldn't fail Josh as he had Bruce. He hadn't stepped in with sympathy or support; he hadn't been there, when his brother had needed him most. He wouldn't make that mistake with Josh. He couldn't lose his best friend as he had his brother. "No, you're not crazy."

Maybe he'd just gotten into the punch. Although the little brass plate on the crystal bowl described it as nonalcoholic, Nick definitely had tasted vodka in the fruity concoction. The alcohol still burned in his stomach but it didn't take the edge off his anger. Right now, he hated Molly McClintock for putting Josh through more pain.

Josh sighed again. "Hell, maybe I am crazy."

"Let's get out of here," Nick suggested.

"Yeah, I better find the boys. I thought they might be in here."

"Think they're flushing something down the toilet?"

Josh shook his head, but Nick doubted he was denying their capacity for naughtiness. Josh knew what hellions his sons were. He got regular reports from the boys' nannies right before they quit working for him. Maybe that was why he'd wanted to get married. But hell, from the way Josh's first wife had walked out on them, he had to know that a second wife could quit, too.

"I'm not talking about leaving just the reception," Nick continued. "I'm talking about this town. Once the office is done we can sell the building and build or lease one closer to the hospital in Grand Rapids."

"The house…"

"You said you don't have possession yet. The seller was probably in church today." Hadn't the whole damn town been there? "He'd understand that you changed your mind. I'm sure you could back out."

"We closed escrow already," Josh said. "And I gave my word."

Once Josh gave his word, he didn't go back on it. Unlike his runaway bride. "Then you can sell it—"

"It needs some work."

Nick shook his head. "Come on, let's get out of Cloverville. There's *nothing* for you here."

"I think there is," Josh insisted, his blue eyes bright with hope. He paused beside Nick and clasped his shoulder. "Maybe there would be for you, too, if you'd give it a chance."

What? The town—or a certain brown-haired bridesmaid? He didn't ask and Josh didn't offer an explanation before his hand slid away and he left.

Nick let the door close behind his friend and walked to the sink to splash water on his own face. He should be relieved that Josh was still so optimistic. Optimism was way better than despair.

Nick acknowledged the fact that he probably didn't have to worry about Josh, but his heart didn't lift with relief. Maybe he wasn't worried about Josh. Maybe he was worried about himself. Because the minute he stepped out of the restroom, he searched the crowded reception hall for her. Colleen, he'd heard her friends call her. She stood with the other brides-maids huddled near the head table where they'd just eaten the most awkward dinner Nick had ever been a part of.

The bride's mom had turned the reception into a wel-come-home party for the blond bridesmaid and her young daughter, and while the guests had enthusiastically greeted the young woman and her child, they'd still had time to stare at Josh. And Nick.

Probably wondering when he was going to blow. How could Josh be so understanding and forgiving? Nick wanted to *hurt* someone.

Chapter Three

Colleen shivered as Nick Jameson approached, passing Abby as she headed away from him, toward the dance floor.

"Do you know Dr. Jameson from the hospital?" Brenna asked. She was one of the few people in Cloverville who knew Colleen volunteered at the hospital in Grand Rapids, but even she didn't know why.

Colleen hadn't actually ever *met* Dr. Jameson. He never acknowledged any of the volunteers, no matter how desperately some of them fought for his attention. "I only know him by reputation."

As a no-nonsense orthopedic surgeon. Not only the volunteers but several of the female staff obsessed over him, longing to experience his "elusive" bedside manner, but Colleen wasn't one of those women who'd considered breaking her leg to get his attention. As he closed the distance between them now, Colleen's pulse quickened. *She* had preferred it when he hadn't noticed her at all.

His gaze moved over her like a caress, lingering on her bare shoulders and the low bodice of her dress. Why look at her meager cleavage when she stood next to a Grecian goddess like Brenna? And yet he didn't even glance at the redhead, although he addressed them both. "Ladies."

"Dr. Jameson," Brenna said. "Have you seen Josh? Is he okay?"

Nick's shoulders twitched stiffly in a tense shrug. "I don't know. He's looking for TJ and Buzz."

Brenna smiled, and her green eyes softened with affection. "The boys are with my parents. I'll let Josh know."

Colleen reached out, trying to catch her friend's arm, but the maid of honor slipped away, leaving Colleen alone with Nick Jameson. He closed his hand around her outstretched one, entwining his long fingers with hers. Colleen drew in a deep breath as indescribable sensations raced through her. She tugged on her hand, but he didn't release her.

"Let's dance," he said, leading her toward the crowded floor before she could sputter out a protest.

And she would have protested. She didn't want to dance with a man who'd called her sister flaky. *Hypocrite.* She didn't want to dance with a man who'd seen her any number of times but had never noticed her before.

Until today. Until she wore the red dress Brenna had picked out for the bridesmaids to wear. Despite the fact that *she* was the bride, Molly had made none of the arrangements for her wedding. Given her apparent disinterest, maybe no one should have been surprised that she'd backed out of the marriage. But Molly wasn't flaky, as Nick had said. Once she set her mind on something, she followed through—like becoming a doctor. While Colleen liked volunteering at the hospital, she would never have been able to handle the studies, as Molly had, taking time off from medical school only for her wedding. Her *wedding-that-wasn't.*

Josh's wedding, too.

"How is the groom?" she asked, as Nick led her in between the other dancing couples and kids to a remote corner of the floor.

"Groom?" he snorted as he pulled her into his arms. "Groom implies that there was a wedding." His jaw taut, he ground out his words. "There was no wedding. There was no bride. So no, there is *no* groom."

Colleen's reluctance to dance with him had nothing to do with her wounded ego. She couldn't dance with a man this angry with her sister. He acted as if *he* were the jilted groom. She stopped moving and tried to pull away, but his hands continued to hold her close.

His breath shuddered out, stirring her hair. "He's my *best* friend." Emotion cracked the deep smoothness of his voice. "I *hate* to see him go through this again."

"Again?" *Oh, God, the poor man…*

"He didn't get left at the altar before. But when the twins were babies, their mom, Josh's first wife, just took off."

Like Molly had. Probably not out a window, but still she'd abandoned her husband and children. Colleen knew what it felt like to be abandoned. Shortly after her dad died, Molly and Brenna had left for college, Eric had enlisted in the Marines and Abby had just…*left.* Colleen had never felt so alone. She lifted her hand to Nick's shoulder and settled back into his arms, moving her feet to follow his lead as the music played, low and smoky. "I'm sorry."

Nick shrugged, muscles rippling beneath her palm. "He says he's staying in Cloverville."

Waiting for Molly. Men waited for Molly. They didn't even notice Colleen. *Usually.*

NICK SHIFTED HIS HAND against her back. Moving his palm over the smooth red satin, he longed to touch her, to see if her skin was as silky as the dress. She was so slender his hand nearly spanned the back of her waist. He nudged her closer, so that she settled against his chest. His pulse leaped as he breathed in the scent of lilies from a small sprig of flowers clasped in her hair. Some of the chocolate-colored strands brushed his chin and throat. He'd never felt anything as soft except for the kitten he'd once bought the twins. But the boys' rambuctiousness had scared the little thing so much he'd had to rescue it from them.

When he tilted Colleen's chin, she stared up at him with enormous dark eyes, as vulnerable and frightened as the kitten had been. Why did she fear him? Did she feel his barely controlled anger over how her sister had humiliated his best friend?

Or did she feel the desire he could hardly control at this moment—for her? "Colleen…"

Something about her, that vulnerability, her youth and air of innocence, suggested she needed rescuing and compelled him to step up and save her. But Nick knew, the only one from whom *he* could save her was himself. His anger still simmered, but he couldn't hurt *her.*

As she blinked, thick black lashes brushed her cheekbones. She had the face of a model, with huge expressive eyes, exquisite cheekbones, delicate nose and generous lips. Kissable lips.

He jerked up his chin, tearing his gaze from her face. Over her head he glimpsed another couple on the dance floor, and watched as the tall man leaned over the petite woman in his arms. Clayton McClintock was kissing the blond bridesmaid with hunger and passion. The way Nick wanted to kiss Colleen.

What the hell was he thinking? Even if her sister hadn't left Josh at the altar, he wouldn't want to get mixed up with some young girl from Cloverville. Small-town women expected commitments. They wanted husbands and kids. He couldn't give Colleen McClintock any of those things. He would never put himself in that position, being so vulnerable to another person. If Josh, if *Bruce,* hadn't picked the right woman to love, how could *he?*

"Dr. Jameson?" she said, her voice soft and tentative rather than haughty as it had seemed at the church. Which voice matched the real woman? Her change in attitude reminded him that he couldn't trust his instincts, not regarding women.

"Use my first name," he told her. He didn't want this woman calling him Doctor. He wanted to hear his name on her lips, but she didn't say a thing. She just stared up at him, those deep eyes so fathomless they were impossible to read. Did she really not know his name? Maybe she didn't. He hadn't known hers, either. "Nick."

"Nick," she repeated, her voice breathless as her gaze held his.

His heart pounded and adrenaline rushed through his veins with the heat of desire. All she had to do was say his name and he nearly forgot his anger at the way her sister had treated Josh.

"Nick." She said his name again. "You were going to tell me something."

That was before he'd been overcome with the urge to kiss her. He drew in a deep breath, remembering his decision. "Since Josh is staying in Cloverville, so am I."

COLLEEN REACHED FOR THE glass of punch she'd left on the head table next to her purse. She hadn't had time to take a sip, for the mingling and the desperate calls she'd been placing to Molly's turned-off cell. And the dancing. She shouldn't have danced with the best man.

Fortunately, the slow song had ended just as he'd told her of his intention to stay in town. She'd been able to pull away without drawing attention to them. Then she'd lost him in the crowd of dancers. Or maybe he hadn't tried to follow her. Why would he? Just because a couple of times he'd leaned forward as if he'd been about to kiss her?

She'd probably only imagined seeing desire in his eyes because she'd had a crush on him for so long. While he didn't have Josh's bedside manner, he was a brilliant surgeon. But more than his medical expertise or his fair-haired good looks, she'd been drawn to the sense of sadness that surrounded him, as if he, too, had experienced loss. In him, she'd felt as if she'd recognized a kindred spirit. But she'd probably only imagined that, too. She and Dr. Nick Jameson were nothing alike, and she needed to get a trip on those feelings she had for him.

She'd impulsively acted on one other crush, a long time ago. But the object of her affection hadn't really wanted her. The arrogant high school jock had only been interested in bragging rights. She'd vowed then to never give herself away again. But why did she suspect that acting impulsively with a man such as Nick Jameson would be infinitely more enjoyable than her youthful experience with a clumsy boy?

Heat, as hot as what she thought she'd glimpsed in Nick's eyes, flashed through her, leaving her parched. Hand shaking, she lifted the plastic cup to her lips. She gulped the red punch, then sputtered and coughed as alcohol burned her throat. Who'd spiked it?

Rory. Blinking tears from her eyes, she scanned the reception hall for her teenage brother. Where was the little jerk? Probably outside smoking.

She headed toward the door, where Abby and Brenna stood, deep in conversation. Guilt ate at Colleen as she took in the distraught brightness of Abby's eyes, the way she nibbled on her bottom lip. Abby hated being back in Cloverville. The whole time she'd been growing up, she couldn't wait to leave. Was Colleen being selfish in still wanting her to move home? Maybe she shouldn't have agreed to help her mother convince her friend to stay. If only Abby and Clayton would stop fighting their feelings for each other…

"Blame it on the wedding," Abby said.

"The wedding-that-wasn't," Colleen murmured. "That's what everyone's calling it." Someone opened the door behind Abby, and cool night air rushed in, soothing Colleen's over-heated skin. Her head cleared slightly, but her emotions grew more muddled. Clayton wasn't the only McClintock who was determined to fight his feelings. Maybe Molly had been as afraid to give herself to someone as Colleen was, and that was why she'd bolted before saying her vows.

"So you think Molly's really okay?" Colleen asked, needing Brenna and Abby's reassurance. Molly must have been really afraid to back out on such an important promise. "That she just needs time like her note said?"

Abby reached into her purse and pulled out her phone, checking for voice mail. "No messages."

Brenna shook her head, tumbling locks of brilliant red hair around her shoulders. "I think she meant that she needed more than a few hours."

Colleen sighed. "She also said she wanted time *alone*. Do you really believe she's alone? When I called Eric, he said he hadn't seen her, but…"

Could they believe Eric, after the way he'd backed out of the wedding party at the last minute? After Molly went out the window, each of the bridesmaids had called him, but he'd sworn he hadn't seen Molly.

"Eric would lie for her," Brenna said.

"He'd do more than lie," Abby reminded them.

Jealousy caused the sweet spiked punch to swirl in Colleen's stomach. Her *first* crush hadn't been on the high school jerk but on Eric South. Yet years ago, during her adolescence, she'd buried that unrequited crush on Eric, as well as her resentment of her brilliant, beautiful older sister. Molly couldn't help being Molly, the one everyone adored. Colleen had long ago accepted that she would never *be* Molly, and like everyone else, she adored her older sister. She didn't resent her. Not anymore.

But just once, would it be too much to ask for someone to adore *her?* Feeling a penetrating stare, she lifted her gaze to *him.*

NICK SWALLOWED HARD, his mouth dry as he held her gaze. He lifted the plastic cup, sniffed the rim, but didn't take a sip from her glass. Her lipstick, deep crimson, marked the cup in the shape of her full lips. She'd drunk the spiked punch. Was she aware that she had? She'd been so distracted that when she'd gone off to huddle with the other bridesmaids, she'd left her purse on the table.

He lifted his gaze from her beaded crimson bag to study the women who stood near the door. They knew where the bride had gone. Women talked to each other. They didn't talk to him. They flirted. They teased. They never talked.

But maybe that was Nick's fault. He never talked to anyone but Josh anymore.

He couldn't lose his best friend the way he'd lost his big brother, for so long the guiding force in Nick's life. Hell, if not for Bruce, Nick wouldn't have had a life. His brother had saved him from the car accident that had claimed their mother's life. Nick had owed him, but he'd let him down. He hadn't been there when Bruce had needed him. He wouldn't make the same mistake with Josh.

For his best friend, Nick would make any sacrifice. He'd

even spend time with the most tempting woman he'd ever met—but only to pump her for information. Finding the groom's runaway bride had become one of Nick's duties, as best man. While he hadn't agreed with much that his friend had said in the bathroom, he acknowledged the fact that Josh needed to talk to Molly. The sooner he did and accepted that she didn't and would never love him, the sooner Josh could put her and Cloverville behind him and move on.

Maybe that space on Michigan Avenue in Grand Rapids was still available. Sure, the rent had been more than the mortgage payments on the building in Cloverville, but they could swing it. Together. Like they'd done everything else.

Nick glanced down at Colleen's nearly empty cup. Had she had enough to, as his dad would say, prime the pump?

"Thinking of mugging me?" a soft voice asked.

Those tense muscles in his neck prompted a grimace as he whipped his head toward her, to where she stood not more than an arm's length away. How had he not noticed her approach, when he'd hardly taken his gaze off her all day?

What was it about her that drew and held his attention? Was it the bright red dress that bared her shoulders and the delicate ridge of her collarbone? Was it the glossiness of her sable hair? Or the warmth and vulnerability in her deep brown eyes?

She stepped closer, as if she doubted he'd heard her over the music and raised voices of the other wedding guests. "Are you?"

His pulse leaped in reaction. She was so damn beautiful that all rational thought fled his mind. All his plans, all his convictions evaporated in the heat of his attraction to her. "What?"

She gestured toward the beaded bag, which he hadn't realized he held. "I didn't figure you for a purse snatcher," she teased, her eyes shining.

"You left it here," he pointed out, "unattended."

"This is Cloverville," she said, as if that explained everything.

He lifted a brow. "And there's no crime in Cloverville?"

"Nothing more serious than my idiot brother and his degenerate friends spiking the punch." She extended her hand, reaching for her bag.

But he held tight. "I can't give this to you."

"What?"

When he fumbled with the rhinestone clasp, she gasped at his audacity. She had no idea how bold he could be, but now he wanted her to know. He wanted her to know *him*.

"I have to take your keys," he insisted. "You can't drink and drive." As a surgeon, he'd seen far too many drunk drivers and the people hurt by them.

"I'm not driving."

"No, you're not," he agreed, as he pulled out her key ring.

"Hey, those are my house keys, too," she protested.

"This is Cloverville. No crime," he said, tossing her words back at her. "I doubt anyone here locks his door."

Colleen opened and then closed her mouth, completely at a loss. Her mother had never locked her front door, and since Colleen still lived at home, she could get inside without a key. But still, he had no right to take her property. No right to tease her.

An urge came over her to tease him back, to make him want her as she'd wanted him for so long. The reckless desire coursed through her veins with all the fire of the spiked punch. Maybe she'd stifled her impetuous nature for too long. Or maybe the punch had loosened her inhibitions. Either way, she couldn't act. She knew the ramifications of impulsive behavior. She always wound up getting hurt or humiliated.

"Give me my keys and my purse," she demanded as she

managed to summon her earlier haughtiness again. But her hand trembled as she held it out.

"I will," he agreed. *Too easily.* "After I walk you home."

She ignored the traitorous leap of her heartbeat and lifted her chin, saying firmly, "I'm not leaving."

"Your blond friend has already left. And there goes the redhead with Josh." He gestured toward the door.

Colleen followed his gaze. Looking like an old married couple, Brenna walked alongside the groom, each of them carrying a sleeping twin. Their seemingly boundless energy was finally spent.

"Abby Hamilton is 'the blonde,'" she informed him, annoyed that he knew no one's name. He'd skipped the rehearsal dinner, of course, so he hadn't officially met anyone. But he could have at least read a program. "And Brenna Kelly is the maid of honor."

"The maid of honor put up Josh and the twins last night," Nick observed.

Yet she could hardly blame Nick for not being invested in the wedding when even the bride hadn't seemed to care about the plans. Colleen nodded. "Brenna put them up at her folks' house, so the groom wouldn't see the bride before the wedding."

Even so catering to superstition hadn't saved them from bad luck.

Nick snorted, probably sharing the same thought. "They've extended their hospitality even longer," he said, as if amazed at their generosity. "He's still staying with the Kellys." His voice turned bitter as he added, "He's waiting for *your sister* to return."

"Molly will come back," she assured him. If she'd ever really left Cloverville, which Colleen doubted. She had to be at Eric's, safe and protected.

Nick's pale green eyes narrowed as he stared at her. "Do you know where she is?"

As Colleen shook her head, her stomach was doing flips from nerves and punch. She really needed to find Rory—the teenager had to learn there were consequences to thoughtless actions. Colleen hadn't been much older than he was now when she'd learned that painful lesson.

NICK HAD LOST HER again…to that place she retreated when all the color drained from her face and her eyes darkened, haunted with regret.

"Come on," he said, taking her by the elbow to guide her toward the exit. "Let's get you some fresh air."

"I'm fine," she insisted.

But she followed his lead, as she had on the dance floor, their steps perfectly in sync.

It occurred to Nick that'd he'd never been as attuned to another person, not even his best friend, and especially not his brother.

"I don't need air, and I don't need you to walk me home." Instead of sounding petulant, she sounded proud. Her voice was strong with spirit and independence.

Nick pushed open the outside door, and Colleen passed by him into the cool night. Crickets chirped in accompaniment to the buzz of fluorescent lights as flood lamps illuminated the parking lot. "But you're leaving."

"As you pointed out," she said, her voice soft, lost, "all my friends have left."

Why did he suddenly suspect it wasn't the first time Colleen McClintock had been left behind? She was younger than her sister and the other bridesmaids. When they'd gone off to college, she would have still been in high school. She was young. Far too young for him. Even though he was only thirty-two, he felt much older. He swallowed back a sigh. And tired. Damn, he was tired. Too many long hours, too many old regrets.

"When you said earlier that you were staying, you made it sound like more than just tonight. Are you really staying in Cloverville?" she asked as they crossed the parking lot.

"Yes." He couldn't leave Josh alone; he'd made that mistake before. "Like Josh, I have the next couple of weeks off." And he didn't intend to let his friend out of his sight until he was sure he was really all right.

"But where are *you* staying? With Josh and the twins staying there, the Kellys don't have any more room. And Cloverville has no hotels," she said, her lips lifting in a satisfied smile. "No inns. No bed and breakfasts."

Nick realized she didn't want him to stay. He shouldn't care. He knew nothing could come of the attraction he felt for her, and not just because she was too young for him.

"Your brother offered me his spare room," Nick said.

She lifted her face toward him, her eyes wide with surprise. "Really? Clayton prefers being alone, or so he claims."

Nick shrugged, uncertain why McClintock had offered him a guest room. "I think he feels responsible for your sister skipping out on the wedding."

She let out a derisive laugh. "That sounds like Clayton—responsible."

"Or guilty."

"That sounds more like me," she murmured, her voice weary with regret.

"What?" he asked, dipping his head closer to hers, to where the lilies had wilted in her hair. "Feeling guilty because you're hiding your sister?"

"*I'm* not hiding Molly."

"But you know where she is?" And who was hiding her.

"Why do you care?" she asked, defensiveness on her sister's behalf hiding her own vulnerability.

He cared because he needed to protect his friend. So why did he feel as if he needed to protect Colleen McClintock, too? "If you're not hiding your sister, what are you feeling guilty about?"

She shook her head. "I don't know why I said that to you. I guess I did have too much punch."

"How old are you?" he wondered aloud.

"Twenty-three."

Too young to be haunted by all the regrets that *he* had. "What do you know about guilt?"

"Too much," she murmured, as she stepped onto the sidewalk and into the shadows cast by the canopy of tree branches overhead.

"Are you like your sister?" he asked as he followed her along the path. Moonlight streaked through the trees and glittered in her eyes as she stared up at him.

"Molly? No, Molly and I are nothing alike," she assured him. She sounded apologetic now, as if she felt she didn't measure up to her older sister. He understood idolizing an older sibling. Maybe if he hadn't idolized his own brother so much, he would have realized that Bruce was in trouble.

While he tried for a teasing tone, his voice betrayed him, going hoarse with emotion as he asked, "So you're not feeling guilty for breaking some poor man's heart into a thousand pieces?"

"Nobody's ever loved me that way," she said, her voice echoing the longing and loneliness he sometimes felt himself…

He shook his head in disbelief, then reached out to take her hand and tug her to a stop. "I knew there was a reason I didn't like this town."

"What?" she asked.

"All the men are fools."

She emitted a laugh, shaky with nerves. "You better hope Clayton didn't overhear you saying that. You'll lose your bed for the night."

He'd rather be in hers. The dangerous thought staggered him. Then *she* staggered him as her hand slid into his hair and pulled his head down to hers. Her lips, soft and sweet, touched his, tentatively at first, and then they moved surely, as passion ignited the air between them.

Nick threw his arm around her, pulling her so close that not a breath separated her body from his. He drew her in, deepening the kiss. His tongue slid between her lips, tasting her, teasing her, full of promise.

Colleen's lips made promises, too, melding against his in a kiss so hot his skin nearly burned. His heart beat hard and fast, blood rushing in his ears and lower, pulsing through his body. He groaned, wanting her so much he hurt.

Pain nagged at the edge of Colleen's pleasure, pulling her away from the intensity of his kiss. Her knees shook and her body trembled all over. She'd never before experienced emotions like these, the fierce desire quivering deep inside her. She wanted him so badly, but the pain deepened, drawing her out of his spell. Her keys—he held them in the hand pressing against her back— dug through the thin material of her dress and into her skin.

That was the price of passion, the price of love. Pain. She knew it well, remembering all the nights she'd listened to her mother cry over her father. Colleen pulled her hand away from his silky hair and wedged it between them, pushing against his chest. Muscles rippled beneath her palm, and his heart pounded hard against it, echoing the furious beat of hers.

She tore her mouth from his, gasping for air. Gasping for words. "Nick…"

His lips slid down her cheek, nipping at her ear before kissing her throat. "Colleen, let me share *your* bed," he murmured.

She steeled her trembling knees and quelled the urges running riot within her body. She'd spun so many fantasies around this man; fantasies she'd considered safe, since she thought they'd never come true. He would never notice her. He would never touch her. Kiss her. Make love to her.

She reached around, pulling her purse and keys from the hand he held against her back. "No. This wasn't what you think…"

She hadn't been thinking at all. She'd only been acting impulsively. She'd worked so hard to overcome that impulsive nature—to act only after she'd considered all the consequences of her actions. But she hadn't considered any consequences when she'd pulled Dr. Nick Jameson down for a kiss. She hadn't realized how much just a brush of her mouth against his could make her want him. Need him.

"You didn't kiss me?" he asked, pulling her back into his arms.

"It was nothing."

Anger flared inside Nick, burning nearly as hot as his desire for her. He'd started this game, wanting to charm her sister's whereabouts out of her. But then she'd blindsided him.

"That was nothing?" he scoffed. "Let me show you…"

A horn blared and tires squealed as a car careened past them, distracting Nick. She pulled away from his arms, her heels clicking against the sidewalk as she ran.

He would have chased her. The passion humming in his veins, the tension hardening his body, compelled him to go after her and persuade her to finish what she'd started between them with her kiss. But he didn't have the strength to do more than watch her run away.

She hadn't had to kiss him to start anything. The moment he'd caught sight of her he'd felt something he'd never felt for any other woman before.

Love.

Chapter Four

Love at first sight. Usually, he'd have scoffed at such a ridiculous notion. But the feeling had held tight, pressing against his chest, stealing his breath, so that he'd had not a moment's rest all night. Recalling her kiss, her soft skin, her soulful eyes and that damned vulnerability that made him think he needed to protect her.

The coffee he'd downed at Clayton's that morning had merely added to his tension, making him edgy. He had to get out of Cloverville. He had to get away from her. Before he did something even stupider than losing his heart. Before he lost his head.

He checked the brass address plate on the porch of the colorful Victorian farmhouse. He'd found the Kellys' house, which was painted yellow with purple and teal trim. Through the screen door drifted the sounds of running footsteps, laughter and then the crash of something breaking. Probably something porcelain or glass. He hoped not valuable. The twins were here.

Josh hadn't been the only one who'd dodged a bullet when his bride had stood him up at the altar, he realized. Nick had dodged his babysitting duty during the bride and groom's honeymoon, as a result. He couldn't believe he'd let Josh coerce him into volunteering for the job. He'd let himself be flattered to think he was the only one Josh would trust with his boys besides his parents.

Josh's folks were on a cruise for their thirty-fifth wedding anniversary. They'd been planning the trip for so long that Josh hadn't allowed them to cancel it, not even for his wedding. Maybe he'd suspected the marriage might not happen. But he'd intended to introduce his bride to his parents during his honeymoon—they'd been going to meet up with the ship in Greece.

Molly McClintock had ruined all of Josh's plans. Like the office in Cloverville. They couldn't do that now. Since Nick couldn't make Josh understand how bad an idea it was, Molly McClintock would have to—when she came home. She had to come home. Now.

Before Nick got in any deeper with her sister. Love at first sight. Really, what the hell had he been thinking?

He lifted his hand, which was shaking slightly, curled it into a fist and rapped his knuckles against the wooden frame of the purple screen door. Several seconds passed, but no one came. He knocked again, harder.

Finally, the redheaded maid of honor greeted him at the door. "Good morning, Nick."

From the flurry of noise inside, he'd have expected that she'd be frazzled. But her hair flowed in freshly brushed waves around her shoulders, which were bare in the cool green sundress she wore. Her eyes, as she met his gaze through the mesh of the screen, were a cool green, too.

"Hi…"

"Brenna," she reminded him. "My name is Brenna."

"Brenna Kelly, yeah, I know." Now. He hadn't really remembered her first name. He'd met so many people the day before.

She arched a brow, obviously skeptical of his claim. Then she turned away from him. "I'll get Josh for you."

"No!"

Her gaze unflinching, she stared him down, through the screen, like his third-grade teacher. If not for Josh, he surely wouldn't have passed that class. Mrs. Hoolihan hadn't bought any of his excuses for not finishing his homework or for the spitballs on the chalkboard and in Sally Kruger's hair.

"I'd like to talk to you." He swallowed. "Brenna."

She pushed open the screen door and stepped out to join him on the porch. Then she crossed her arms over her ample bosom and waited for him to say more. Despite walking down the aisle together yesterday, they hadn't exchanged more than a few words.

Nick wasn't sure which approach might work with her, but he doubted she'd appreciate his limited charm. Since she seemed straightforward, he opted for being blunt. "You need to tell your friend to come home."

"What?"   .

"You know where the runaway bride is."

"She asked for some time alone," she said, reminding him of the note that Molly had left. Not for the groom she'd hurt and humiliated, but for one of her bridesmaids, Abby Hamilton. He'd advised Clayton to work on Abby, to make her tell him where Molly had gone.

He appreciated that Brenna hadn't lied to him and denied knowing where her friend was. He was right—she was straightforward. "Don't you think that's pretty damned selfish of her?"

Her voice sharpened. "You obviously don't know Molly. She is probably the least selfish person I know."

"I *don't* know her," he admitted. "She was supposed to marry my best friend, and I barely know her name."

"Well, you're bad with names."

He laughed to realize she was aware of one of his quirks. "Josh has been talking to you."

She nodded.

"That's good." That meant he wasn't shutting himself down; he wasn't hiding out alone and drinking himself into oblivion. But then Josh was nothing like Nick's brother. He was stronger than that—he had the boys depending on him. He was their only parent.

If something happened to him, Nick would get custody of the boys. He was their godfather, and because he was younger and more energetic than their grandparents he would become their legal guardian if anything happened to Josh. Nothing could happen to Josh.

The boys deserved better than Nick. They deserved their father—someone who could protect them from all harm.

Her husky voice softened as she acknowledged, "You're worried about him."

"Yes, I am," he admitted. Probably more worried than he had reason to be. "He's determined to talk to her and work things out."

Even though Josh hadn't accepted the fact, Nick was certain they couldn't work out anything. If the woman loved him, she wouldn't have deserted him at the altar. "So you need to tell your friend to come home."

"Molly. Her name is Molly."

"I know her name." He wasn't likely to forget it since she'd hurt his best friend. He remembered Josh's first wife, too, but he didn't often say her name or even think it. "I wish Josh would forget. I wish he'd forget all about her."

Brenna drew in a quick breath, as if startled. "Then I don't understand why you want her to come home."

"*He* can't forget her until he talks to her."

Brenna's lips curved into a rueful smile. "You really don't know Molly. Men don't forget Molly. Seeing her again isn't going to get him to change his mind about moving here or about opening the office that I know you were against opening here. Bringing Molly back won't get you what you want."

"This isn't about what I want." He pushed his hand through his hair. "No, it *is*. I want my friend to be happy. If moving to Cloverville makes him happy, I'll go along with it. I just I want Josh to be *happy*."

Brenna's eyes warmed. "Now I understand."

"What?"

"Why you're his best friend. Now I understand."

Nick nodded. "I am his best friend."

Brenna's head bobbed, too. "I'm Molly's best friend, you know. She wants time alone, and she's getting time alone. I'm not telling you where she is."

He'd been crazy to try to manipulate the maid of honor. He should have known better than to doubt her loyalty. Maybe he'd have better luck with the little sister.

He wouldn't let down Josh as he had Bruce. It didn't matter what he lost along the way, his head or his heart, as long as he didn't lose his best friend.

COLLEEN WANTED TO BLAME the punch for what she'd done the night before, but she hadn't drunk enough of it to excuse her reckless behavior. She stared up at the statue of the Civil War hero who'd come north after the war and founded Cloverville. Colonel Clover stood sentinel in the middle of the town park, leaning forward at an odd angle, his metal body bent and broken. The consequences of her last reckless action. Until last night. Until she'd kissed Dr. Nick Jameson.

She couldn't blame it on the punch. But she could blame *him*. For finally noticing her. For complimenting her in the moonlight. She pressed her palms against her eyes and shook her head. Hadn't she changed at all from the shy teenager who'd fallen for the high school jock because he'd paid her the slightest bit of attention? Giving up her virginity to that jerk hadn't been reckless or even impulsive— it had been stupid. Surely she was smarter than that insecure kid she used to be. Now she knew when a man was after something.

Footsteps trampled the grass behind her, but she didn't bother to turn, expecting Mr. Meisner and his dog. He was usually the only other person in the park this early in the morning.

"Man, Cloverville is pretty twisted if this 'statue' is supposed to be a tribute to the town founder."

She tensed but didn't turn toward the intruder as her face heated with embarrassment. "He didn't always look like that."

"I'd hate to see the other guy."

As the "other guy," Colleen had ended up with some scratches and bruises from the broken windshield and the steering wheel. Unfortunately, Abby's car had been too old for airbags. While her scratches had healed and her bruises had faded, Colleen still bore scars in her heart and her conscience. Abby had insisted on taking the blame for the damage to the colonel, and Colleen had let her do it. She never should have agreed. She should have told the truth, even though Abby had probably been right that no one would have believed her anyway.

She'd always been perceived as innocent little Colleen, which was why the jerk jock had targeted her. She'd been a challenge. She suspected Nick saw her as a challenge, too, but he wasn't after her innocence. He was after her sister.

"So is the park the first stop on your tour of all Cloverville's attractions?" she asked, managing to summon the haughty tone she'd used the first time they'd spoken.

He emitted an amused chuckle. "Attractions? There's more than one? Now I really regret not signing up for the tour."

"Did you just stumble on the colonel by accident?" The same way she'd broken the statue.

"No, I'm here because your mother told me where I could find you."

Even though she knew he had ulterior motives, her pulse quickened with excitement simply because he'd sought her out. Then Colleen closed her eyes, imagining the spark of matchmaking glee that had surely warmed her mother's heart. Oh, she wouldn't hear the end of the handsome doctor coming to see her anytime soon. Her mother would increase the pressure for marriage and procreation. Colleen's shoulders drooped in anticipation.

"So you wanted to talk to me?" she asked, the disdain gone, replaced by a quaver of nerves. Did he want to talk or was he more interested in finishing what she'd started the night before? And if it were the latter, was she strong enough to resist him?

"You are like your sister, you know," he mused.

She turned then, opening her eyes to study him. Even in his rumpled tuxedo pants and wrinkled pleated shirt, Dr. Nick Jameson was devastatingly handsome. "You don't know either one of us."

And yet he was Molly's fiancé's best friend. How was it that this man didn't know her sister, that he didn't understand that Molly wouldn't deliberately hurt another human being? She was too sweet and generous.

"I know that both of the McClintock women make promises," he said, his pale eyes gleaming as he stepped closer to her, "then run off without a word of explanation for breaking them."

"Promises?" Her head pounded as she furrowed her brows in confusion. "I never made you any promises."

He touched her lips, sliding his thumb back and forth across her bottom one. Her breath backed up in her lungs. She couldn't exhale; she couldn't move. She could only stand there and let him touch her.

"You made me a promise, Colleen," he said, "when you kissed me."

She stepped back, and his hand dropped away. Then she shook her head. "I had too much punch." She wished that was the reason she'd kissed him—that she'd been drunk. But she didn't have an excuse, even a bad one.

"You kept insisting to me that you were fine," he reminded her. "And you were, Colleen. Your kiss…"

She pressed her fingers over his mouth now. She didn't need any reminders of her reckless behavior. She already had the colonel.

But he didn't stop talking, moving his lips against her fingers, blowing softly against her skin. "Colleen, *you* kissed *me*, and you weren't drunk. So why? *Why* did you kiss me?"

Her fingers tingling, she pulled away her hand and clenched it at her side. "Blame it on the moonlight."

Her parents used to dance to a song with that title, by some obscure old singer—she'd only heard it when they'd played the record. She could close her eyes and remember watching from the stairs as her dad had twirled her mother around the living room. They hadn't seen her, had had no idea she'd snuck out of bed, prompted by the music.

Nick hummed a few bars of the tune, one of his father's favorites, as well. But when Colleen opened her eyes again and he glimpsed her tears, he wished he hadn't.

"Colleen, what's wrong? What did I say?"

"Uncle Nick! Uncle Nick!" shouted one of the twins. "Buzz is turning green!"

He closed his eyes and winced. Maybe trusting them to push each other on the merry-go-round hadn't been such a good idea. "I'm coming!" he shouted.

"You have the boys?" she asked, as she followed him across the wood chips that blanketed the playground area of the park.

"Yeah." Even in a small, safe town like Cloverville, he'd been careful to keep them in sight, but he still hadn't been paying enough attention. He'd been distracted. *She'd* distracted him.

"All by yourself?" she asked, her head turning to scan the empty park.

"Yes." He should have been offended, given that she obviously didn't think he was capable of handling the boys on his own. But even though he'd agreed to babysit—and to become guardian if, God forbid, something happened to Josh—he had his doubts, too.

He reached the merry-go-round and caught TJ, who'd been spinning his brother, around his waist. Then he reached out, catching the metal supports as they flew past, and slowed down the whirling ride.

"Hey, buddy, you okay?" he asked Buzz, who had definitely turned a pea-soup shade of green.

"I don't feel so good, Uncle Nick," Buzz murmured as he crawled out from the middle. Before his wobbly legs touched the ground, Nick lifted him up, and now he had a twin under each arm.

"Okay, guys, let's take a break for a minute," he said as he carried the boys toward the grass.

TJ squirmed. "Hey, I want to play. I want to play."

And if he played, Buzz would try to keep up with him, no matter how sick the poor kid felt.

"You were pushing hard," Nick reminded TJ. He'd no doubt been pushing hard to try to dislodge his brother from the merry-go-round—the boys constantly competed with each other.

Nick didn't understand sibling rivalry. His brother had been ten years older. So his only real competition growing up had been Josh, and since his best friend was such a nice guy, he'd never minded losing to him.

He told TJ, "You need to catch your breath."

And Buzz needed to find his. The poor kid still hung like a limp noodle from Nick's arm. Nick dropped down onto the grass, keeping both boys close. Buzz rolled onto his stomach, resting his head on Nick's thigh.

"I wanna play, too," he muttered weakly, his drool soaking through Nick's tux pants.

Nick ran his hand over the little guy's buzzed head, which was soft and warm—too warm—against Nick's palm. "I know. You want to play, too."

Buzz would never admit defeat to his brother.

TJ wriggled, trying to loosen Nick's grip. "C'mon, lemme go. I don't wanna sit down."

"Just for a little while," Nick promised, and then looked up at Colleen, who joined them carrying a backpack. Yesterday she'd worn a floor-length gown, so he hadn't noticed how long and sexy her legs were, but now they were bared by brief denim shorts. As she settled onto the grass, she folded her legs beneath her.

Nick sucked in a breath, surprised by the small butterfly tattoo that adorned the side of one delicate ankle. The bright-colored wings spread wide, as if the butterfly were in midflight.

"Pretty," TJ said, reaching out to rub a sticky finger across the tattoo.

Colleen turned and laughed, and her whole face was illuminated. Jealousy churned Nick's stomach. Was he really jealous of a four-year-old for touching her and making her laugh? Probably. Damn, he'd never been the possessive type. Not even with the women he'd actually dated. And he really had no intention of dating Colleen McClintock—only prying information out of her. Since her sister couldn't be trusted, no doubt she couldn't be, either.

"Thank you," she told TJ. "I have a few things in here you guys might like."

She definitely had a few things Nick liked.

"Crackers," she said, handing a box to Nick to open. "And a book. Would you both like to hear a story?" She drew a picture book from her pack.

"Is that Lara's book?" TJ asked, wrinkling his nose in disgust. "I don't want to read about Barbies or princesses." Obviously, he was referring to the flower girl, who was Colleen's houseguest.

Nick opened his mouth to launch into the lecture on manners that he'd heard often enough while growing up. If he believed his father, he'd been as much of a handful as the twins were. "TJ…"

"It's about slaying dragons," Colleen assured the boys. Actually, it was about a princess who slew her own dragons. But when Colleen read the story, infusing such emotion into the tale as she voiced each character's part, the boys were enthralled. And quiet and still. Two things Nick hadn't known they could be. The problem was that he was enthralled, too. Not with the story, but with Colleen McClintock.

Nick's reprieve with the boys lasted only until Colleen uttered those fateful words, "The End." Then Buzz, finally recovered from the merry-go-round, sprang to his feet and pointed. "Look, there's a puppy. Can we go see the puppy, Uncle Nick?"

Nick craned his neck in the direction of an old man who was leading a dog that clearly hadn't been a puppy for a long time. "Wait, boys!"

Before he could leap to his feet, Colleen's hand brushed against his thigh. His muscles contracted beneath her palm and he had to catch his breath.

"It's okay," she assured him, as she swept cracker crumbs from his pants. "Ol' Lolly doesn't bite." From the way she pulled her hand back and replaced it in her lap, however, maybe she thought he would.

And, man, she tempted him.

"But the boys…" Had terrified that poor kitten he'd brought them. But not Colleen. She'd handled the twins better than he could have imagined. If Josh had just been looking for a mother for his sons, he'd probably proposed to the wrong McClintock sister. Nick's gut tightened, his jealousy for the father instead of the sons this time. He didn't want to imagine Josh kissing Colleen, touching her. He could imagine only one man holding her the way a man held a woman he loved. Himself.

"Lolly is so old she barely has any teeth left," Colleen continued. "The boys are safe."

Maybe the boys were okay, but Nick wasn't so sure about himself.

"You were brave to bring them to the park by yourself," she mused as she packed up the book and the leftover crackers in her backpack.

He laughed. "More stupid than brave." How had he intended to talk to her with the boys around? He hadn't been worried about talking, though. He'd been focusing on what else he might have done with Colleen if he'd come to see her without his twin chaperones. But the presence of TJ and Buzz hadn't mattered; she'd still gotten to him more than he had to her. "I don't know how I thought I could have managed them on my own for two weeks."

"What?"

"I was supposed to take care of them while Josh was on his honeymoon," he explained. "So I guess I really owe your sister a thank-you."

"Nick!" she admonished.

At least she didn't take lightly the fact that her sister had left her groom at the altar, humiliated in front of their guests. And if she didn't approve, maybe she would share Molly's whereabouts. He could have flat out asked her, as he'd asked Brenna, but with Colleen he figured finesse might work better than bluntness.

"But since I can't thank her—" yet "—I'll thank you. Meet me back here this afternoon," he said. "I'll pay you back for the crackers and the story."

COLLEEN DIDN'T WANT ANYTHING from Nick Jameson—she didn't trust him. His interest in her couldn't be genuine. But she was enormously flattered that he wanted to see more of her. She bit her lip, reminding herself of what had happened the last time a guy had flattered her. She'd ended up hurt and humiliated and she'd given away something she could never get back. Her innocence. She feared Nick could take more than that from her. Her heart. She stood up and turned away from him, toward the boys, gesturing to the one with the shorter hair. "He sure recovered fast."

"Yes," Nick agreed with a weary-sounding sigh as he hauled himself to his feet.

Kids were so much more resilient than adults. Rory, being the youngest of the McClintock's, had handled his father's death the easiest of all the siblings. Or so Colleen had thought until he'd started smoking and spiking punch bowls. "What's his name?"

His voice warm with affection, Nick answered, "That's Buzz."

She laughed. "I know, and understand *why* he's called Buzz, but what's his real name?"

"Nicholas James, and TJ is Thomas." His voice warmed even more as he stepped closer, his body nearly brushing her back. "Thomas, for my dad, and Joshua, for Josh's. Josh is named after his dad, too, and he didn't want his son to be a third. Not since the kid's already a double."

"You and Josh go back a long way," she said as she stepped forward, edging away from the heat of his body. "You're really close."

"Yes." He followed her, eliminating the small space her step had put between them.

"You'd do anything for him, wouldn't you?" Or anyone. That was why he'd turned on the charm with her, when for so long he hadn't even noticed her. Apparently even before Molly had disappeared, he'd been looking out for the groom's best interests. That was why he'd finally begun to pay attention to her, after all those years of staring straight through her as if she didn't exist.

In her mind—the only place where she entertained reckless actions she never intended to carry out—she'd often fantasized about him finally noticing her. He'd glance up one day when they passed in the hall or as he sat at a table in the cafeteria, and he'd see her across from him and tell her she was so beautiful that he had to have her. No other woman would ever do.

She forced away all such thoughts now, manifestations of her unrequited crush, and focused on his real reason for paying attention to her. "You're such close friends that you're even staying in Cloverville for him."

"Maybe I'm not staying for Josh," he said as his hand settled at the side of her waist, where her shirt had ridden up above her shorts. His palm warmed her bare skin.

"You're not staying for me," she insisted. She had nothing to offer him. She would not betray her sister.

"Don't sell yourself short," he said, leaning close so that his breath stirred the hair against her neck. "From what I can tell, you're the *only* attraction in Cloverville."

Attraction. She wished that were all this was, this compelling emotion that shimmered like midsummer humidity in the air between them. Despite the heat of his touch, she shivered. "I'm not an attraction, Nick."

"You are, for me." He pulled her closer, so that her back settled against the hard muscles of his chest. So that she touched him from her head to her heels, and felt his body taut and warm against hers.

She turned and her face suddenly brushed his throat, where his pulse pounded madly.

"Nick," she murmured in protest of the way he made her feel. Weak. Dizzy. As if she'd been the one TJ had spun on the merry-go-round instead of his twin.

"God, Colleen, I wish we were alone," he said, his hand tightening on her hip, pulling her closer for just a moment before he groaned and set her away from him.

"Please meet me back here at two," he urged, his voice thick with desire. "I'll bring the picnic lunch."

She didn't answer Nick, but he walked off as if she'd agreed. Had a woman ever turned him down? She doubted it.

He rescued Lolly from the boys. Buzz and TJ turned back to wave at her before leaving the park with Nick, each of them holding one of his hands. If she hadn't seen it with her own eyes, she wouldn't have believed how good he was with the twins. At the hospital, his intention to remain single was a legend. What a waste.

Her heart would be wasted, too, if she fell for Nick Jameson. His picnic invitation might be tempting, but she had to resist.

Chapter Five

"You're sure you're okay with me staying here?" Nick asked as he dropped his duffel bag onto the polished hardwood floor of Clayton McClintock's apartment, a loft above his insurance agency. He placed the picnic basket atop the marble counter-top, careful not to knock around the contents inside. He didn't want to break the wine bottle. "No hard feelings over our not leasing your open space downstairs?"

That had been his decision more than Josh's. While the commercial space had been okay for a one-doctor private practice, Nick and Josh needed more room for the two of them and the physical therapist they intended to hire.

Clayton shook his head. "No. I understand that you need more room than Dr. Strover. And you're more than welcome to stay here."

But Nick could tell from the quizzical tone in his host's voice that Clayton wondered *why* Nick wanted to stay. Clover-ville was just a little over an hour's drive from Grand Rapids. But an hour away would be too far if Josh suddenly needed him. Bruce hadn't been that far away, and Nick still hadn't managed to get to him in time.

If only he'd been able to talk Josh into leaving Cloverville right away, then he wouldn't have to stay. But Nick suspected the only person who'd be able to talk Josh into leaving was his runaway bride. Nick had to find her, and soon—before he put himself at risk.

"Thanks for the hospitality." He offered his host gratitude but not an explanation. He'd always been guarded about his personal history, about his pain.

"You didn't have to bring me anything," Clayton said, gesturing toward the picnic basket as he leaned against the front of the walnut kitchen cabinets.

Nick laughed. "I appreciate you letting me stay here, but this isn't for you."

He'd picked up the basket at his favorite deli in Grand Rapids, when he'd gone back to his condo to pack a few things. He was hoping he wouldn't be here long enough to wear everything he'd brought with him, but the tux wasn't his. He'd had to drop it off at the rental place, grass stains, Buzz drool and all.

"Hot date?"

Somehow Nick suspected that Clayton, the protective older brother, would not appreciate Nick seeing Colleen. At least not as Nick saw her. Hell, he knew he was too old for her, too cynical, that he had nothing to offer her. He didn't need Clayton McClintock to tell him what he already knew. Doubting that he'd have a place to stay at all if Clayton were aware of his date's identity, Nick shook his head. "How about you? Did you talk to your girlfriend this morning?"

After a restless night in the guest room, Nick had come out of the kitchen at the crack of dawn to find Clayton watching his blond bridesmaid through the living-room blinds. He'd pointed out then that the bridesmaids knew where the bride had run off to, and he'd urged Clayton to find his missing sister—and not just for Josh but to make sure she was okay.

"Abby Hamilton is not my girlfriend," Clayton hotly denied, just as he had when Nick had asked him that morning. "But I did talk to her."

Suppressing a grin at the other man's vehement reaction, Nick amended his question. "Did you get through to Abby?"

"No, there's no getting through to Abby Hamilton."

"Stubborn, huh?"

"Aggravating. Frustrating." Clayton groaned.

The man had it bad. Nick's best friend had been engaged twice, married once, and he'd never talked about either woman with as much emotion as Clayton showed for Abby Hamilton or as Nick had invested in Colleen McClintock.

"It's okay, though," Clayton said, apparently to reassure himself. "She won't stick around Cloverville."

"I bet she'll be here until your sister comes back." Old memories stepped out of the shadows of Nick's mind. "If she comes back…" His brother had never come back, not after his wife left him. Nick always thought that in some ways Bruce had really died that day, long before his car had struck the tree.

"Molly will come back."

"Why?" Nick couldn't imagine why anyone would willingly return to Cloverville once they'd left. Then images began to flash through his mind—of Colleen in her strapless dress standing on the sidewalk in the moonlight, and then in the park on the grass next to him, her long bare legs folded beneath her, her beautiful face animated as she read to the boys. She shouldn't be that compelling of an attraction; she shouldn't mean that much to him already.

He gripped the handle of his basket. He should *not* go back to the park. He doubted he'd get any information out of her, but he might give up more than he'd ever intended to give anyone—his heart.

"You're a city snob, huh?"

"What?"

"You can't live outside a city? We're not that far from Grand Rapids, you know." Clayton's voice vibrated with pride in his town.

"Seems like a lot more than an hour," Nick said. Maybe because only a two-lane highway connected the cities, rather than a freeway, and the only scenery between the two places was fields and woods. "While you're half right, I'm no snob."

He'd worked his way through school. As a welder, his dad had barely made ends meet for his family. He hadn't been able to help Nick. "But I have always lived in cities. In fact, Grand Rapids seems small to me. Josh and I grew up in Detroit."

"Detroit?" Clayton whistled. "Yeah, Cloverville must seem like not much more than a dot on a map to you."

"It has a dot?" he teased.

Clayton grinned. "I think if you really look you'll find that it has a lot to offer."

Again Colleen's image sprang to Nick's mind, her face alive with warmth and humor as she laughed at TJ. He closed his eyes, but then he could hear her, reading the silly story, her voice soft but vibrant.

Clayton's knuckles, rapping against the wooden cover of the basket, drew Nick's attention back. "Or maybe you've already figured that out."

The only thing Nick had figured out was that he was in trouble. For the first time since he was a teenager, he'd lost his focus. "No, there's nothing here for me."

"You're opening an office here," Clayton pointed out.

"Maybe that'll change." He hoped like hell it would. "Josh needs to talk to your sister."

"She'll come home," her older brother assured him. "There's a lot in Cloverville for Molly. Her friends. Her family."

Nick nodded. "I know family and friends are important. So you're not worried about her?"

Clayton shook his head. "No. Molly's smart and real level-headed."

Nick lifted a brow. He hadn't seen much to support Clayton's opinion of Molly McClintock. But Nick understood seeing a sibling as you wanted them to be, instead of how they really were. He'd always idolized his older brother. But Clayton *was* the older brother; he should have a little more objectivity than Colleen might.

Clayton laughed. "You might find that hard to believe right now, but Molly's quite responsible. She'd never…"

"Back out on a promise?"

"She has a good reason," her loyal brother insisted. "You'll see."

Nick bit his tongue, holding back a rant about how she'd hurt and humiliated the man she'd promised to marry. Siblings might insult each other, but they didn't let outsiders talk that way. Despite their friendship, Nick had once blackened Josh's eye over his brother. It was a wonder they were still friends.

Nick owed Josh so much. If he hadn't been there for Nick, helping him focus after the grief and guilt over how he'd lost his brother, he shuddered to think what he might have become. He'd started drinking and picking fights—he would have probably wound up like Bruce, dead too young—if Josh hadn't pulled him back from the depths of his grief and guilt.

"You're sure Molly's okay?" Nick asked. He figured Clayton, who'd taken on so much responsibility when his dad died, would never forgive himself if something happened to Molly.

Clayton nodded. "She would never do anything crazy."

She went out a window on her wedding day, but maybe that was a smart thing. Running instead of committing. Nick glanced down at the picnic basket. If he were smart, he'd run, too. Far away from Colleen McClintock.

COLLEEN PULLED OPEN THE screen door and walked into the Kellys' house. They would have been offended if she'd knocked. She'd spent so much time at the Kellys' when she'd been growing up—especially after her dad died. Even though Brenna had been away at college in central Michigan, her parents had continued to welcome Colleen's visits. They'd always wanted lots of children, but they hadn't had Brenna until they were in their forties.

Colleen thought that her mother put too much pressure on Clayton and her for grandchildren. She couldn't imagine how much pressure the Kellys must exert on Brenna.

"Hey, Brenna!" she called into the quiet house. Too quiet, really, if the boys were still staying with the Kellys.

And if they weren't, that meant that Josh had changed his mind about staying in Cloverville. And if he wasn't staying, neither would Nick. She told herself she should feel relief, but it wasn't relief that was pressing hard on her chest, making her breathing difficult.

Nick must be gone.

Sure, she could see him at the hospital. But *he* wouldn't see her there. He never had. She swallowed hard, then called out again. "Hello?"

A clatter rang out from the kitchen, as if pans were dropping on the hardwood floor. A smile formed on her lips; everyone was always in the kitchen at the Kellys'. It was usually that way at her house, too. She walked through the parlor, with its polished antiques, down the hall to the kitchen. "Hey!"

Joshua Towers stood by the center island of the gourmet kitchen, its state-of-the-art appliances were totally at odds with the rest of the Victorian house. Josh leaned forward, his palms pressed flat against the granite counter. His black hair rose up in tufts, as if he'd been running his hands through it.

"Are you okay?" Guilt swirled through Colleen. She recognized the feeling instantly because she'd lived with it for so long. Sure, she hadn't stood him up—but her sister had. Maybe she was a little like Clayton after all, assuming responsibility for other people's actions.

Josh sighed. "Yeah, sure."

Colleen stepped forward, her foot sending a frying pan spinning into the side of the island. She leaned over and picked it up.

"It must have fallen," Josh murmured, gesturing toward the pot rack, which hung over the island, swaying slightly on its chains.

She placed the pan in the industrial-size stainless-steel sink. "Where is everyone?" she asked.

"Mr. and Mrs. Kelly took the boys into town."

Probably to protect their antiques. But actually the Kellys weren't like that. People meant more to them than possessions did. Still, the house had made some of their group of friends uncomfortable. Eric and Abby always had preferred the McClintock house to the Kellys'. They'd said it was because they hadn't had to worry about breaking things there.

But everything Colleen had ever cared about had broken in that house. Her family. Her heart.

"And Brenna, where is she?" she asked. She needed to talk to someone.

Colleen would have talked to Abby, but when she'd gone home after the park, the house had been empty. She'd checked her bedroom to see if Molly had returned. Despite Clayton's room usually being empty—when Abby wasn't staying in it—Molly still shared their old bedroom when she wasn't away at school. But her sister still hadn't come home, and a note held with a magnet on the refrigerator door explained that her mom had taken Rory, Abby and Lara out for Sunday brunch. They would have waited for her, but Rory had been starving. As usual.

"Uh, Brenna had to… Brenna went upstairs, I think," Josh stammered.

She narrowed her eyes and studied the doctor's handsome face. Tension held his jaw taut and clouded his blue eyes. "Is everything okay *here?*"

Josh's gaze slid away from hers. "Uh…"

"Because if it's not, you and the boys can stay with us," she offered. "Rory can sleep in the family room." He wouldn't be happy about it, but her brother deserved some sort of punishment for spiking the punch at the wedding. Their mom spoiled her "baby" entirely too much. "It's really not a problem. If not for the superstition, my mother would have had you stay with us anyway."

"Maybe she was right to be superstitious."

"So you saw Molly before the wedding?" Colleen had wondered if Josh hadn't had some inkling that Molly might flee. He hadn't seemed entirely surprised—or upset—that she'd abandoned him at the altar. And during their slumber party the night before the wedding, Molly had disappeared for a while. When she returned, she claimed she'd just gone outside for some air. But she'd been gone long enough to walk over to the Kellys'.

His face flushed with embarrassment, darkening his tanned skin. "Uh…"

"I'm sorry. I don't mean to pry." She had no right seeking

out other people's secrets when she'd guarded hers for so many years.

"She's your sister. You're not prying. Really," he insisted, as nice and generous as ever.

She suppressed a wistful sigh, totally understanding how Molly could have fallen so quickly for a man like him. Molly had always been the smart one. Too bad Colleen had never gone for the "nice" guys. But then maybe Molly hadn't really fallen for him. "She is my sister. I thought I knew her pretty well. It isn't like Molly to take off the way she did, without any warning."

That was more like Colleen.

"She didn't," Josh assured her. "I mean…I had some warning."

"You knew she might change her mind?"

Footsteps sounded overhead, a door closed. What was Brenna doing? Not being particularly hospitable to her house-guest. That was so unlike Brenna, who'd always been the surrogate mother of their group, taking care of everyone else.

His chin pointing up, he focused on the pressed-tin ceiling. "I knew."

"Then why…" Hadn't he or Molly canceled the wedding?

His broad shoulders lifted and dropped in a brief shrug.

"You don't want to talk about it," she guessed. "I understand."

"That makes one person."

"What? Is someone pressuring you?" She remembered his best friend. "Oh. Nick."

"Yes. Nick." Josh pushed a hand through his already tousled hair in a gesture reminiscent of his best friend's. "He doesn't understand."

"I'm sorry. I know he's your best friend, but…"

"He means well," Josh defended him. "He may not understand me, but I think I understand him. We go back a long way. He loves me like a brother." Josh sighed. "That's why he's pressuring me to leave Cloverville. He's worried that I might do something crazy."

"I thought he considered staying in Cloverville crazy." Colleen's pulse quickened, as she thought of their picnic date. She glanced at her watch. She was supposed to meet him in less than an hour. Actually, she'd never agreed. He'd just assumed that no female could say no to Dr. Nick Jameson, one of the *GQ* doctors. The two men were called other nicknames, too—she'd heard Nick referred to as Dr. Yummy and Dr. Hottie.

But she'd never paid much attention to what the staff and volunteers called Josh. She'd only paid attention to Nick— even when he hadn't noticed she was alive. Or maybe because of that. Because *unrequited* crushes were safe. Picnic dates in the park were not.

"Oh, God," Josh said with a groan. "I'm not the only one he's pressuring. I saw the two of you on the dance floor last night. I should have known what he was up to."

"That he only asked me to dance to find out where my sister is?" She'd known that, of course, but still her face heated with embarrassment and regret dimmed her spirit as, outside the patio doors, clouds rolled across the sun.

"I didn't mean *that*." He shook his head, as if in self-disgust. "That didn't sound right. But you have to know Nick. He's really single-minded."

"I know." He was determined to find her sister.

"No, Colleen, you don't know him. No matter how many years you've been volunteering at the hospital, you don't know Nick," Josh insisted. "He lets very few people get close to him."

"You."

"Like I said, we go back a long way. I knew him before…" Josh sighed. "I knew him before he got like this."

Her breath caught. Had Nick been hurt? "Like *this?*"

"Determined to go it alone, to never get involved with *anyone.*"

"I know," she assured him. "I have been volunteering at the hospital for a few years now. I've heard all the gossip about Dr. Jameson."

Josh nodded. "The sad part is that all the rumors are true. He's never really had a serious relationship."

"I understand not wanting to fall in love. The risk is too great." She didn't want to wind up like her mother, heart-broken and alone.

Josh laughed. "Yeah, he has a point. Hell, with my divorce—now this—I'm probably part of the reason he keeps his relationships casual."

"Part of the reason? What's the other part?" she asked, curiosity overwhelming her good manners. With Nick, she had to pry. "Did he have his heart broken once?"

Josh shook his head. "No. He declared himself a bachelor for life a long time ago."

She nodded. "I see." Although she wasn't sure that she did.

"I know a lot of the nurses and volunteers hope he'll change his mind and date someone from the hospital."

"He doesn't even date?" Then what was the picnic about?

Josh laughed. "He dates. I call it serial dating. Never more than a few times, and never someone he'd risk running into every day."

Then why had he asked her out? Did he have no idea she volunteered at the hospital, or was finding out where Molly was worth the risk of seeing Colleen again—after he'd dumped her and broken her heart?

His blue eyes soft with concern and his voice gentle as if he spoke to one of his boys, Josh said, "Colleen…"

She understood now how he'd earned his reputation as the doctor with the best bedside manner.

"I would hate to see you get hurt," he said. "Trust me—it's no fun."

"I'm not going to get hurt," she assured him. "I don't want to date Nick." Not that she hadn't thought about it, dreamed about it. But fantasies were safe, whereas reality was not. She had no intention of meeting Nick Jameson in the park.

"That's too bad," he said heavily.

A laugh sputtered out of her in reaction to his disappointment. "But I thought you didn't want me getting hurt."

"I don't." His blue eyes narrowed as he studied her face. "But maybe you wouldn't. Maybe you'd be the one who finally got Nick to fall."

"But you said he's determined to never get serious about anyone," she reminded him.

"He made his decision with all the arrogance," Josh laughed, "and ignorance of a man who's never fallen in love. But he will fall one day. And when he does, it's going to be hard, Colleen."

She smiled, and then shook her head. "Maybe. But it won't be for me."

Josh narrowed his eyes and stared at her. "I think you're wrong. I think you're just the kind of woman, sweet and generous, that Nick could finally fall for."

"I've been working at the hospital for so long," she said, even though he'd made the same point only moments ago, "but Nick never noticed me until the wedding."

"Well, yeah, that's because he never dates anyone from the hospital."

"Just like he never gets serious about anyone." She wasn't going to waste her heart on another playboy. From working for Clayton at the insurance agency, she'd learned plenty about risk. And Nick was too great a risk—for her heart. "He's not going to fall for me."

"But I've never seen him look at anyone the way he looked at you yesterday."

Her pulse leaped, but she quelled the excitement. It didn't matter. "I'm not going to fall for him."

"Well…"

"I'm sorry," she said.

"I wish you'd reconsider. Nick's really a great guy. No one could have a more loyal friend," Josh insisted with such vehemence that a muscle jumped in his cheek.

"No. I'm sorry that my sister stood you up at the altar," she explained. "I would have liked having you as my brother-in-law."

He smiled. "We don't have to be family to be friends, Colleen. I'd still like to have you as a friend."

Sadness touched her heart. She hadn't always been the best friend, but she'd learned from her mistakes. "I'd like that too, Josh."

"Good," he said with satisfaction. "I'm going to need friends here. I've already bought a house in Cloverville. For me and the boys."

"You're staying."

"Nick's not happy about it," he said, with a shrug of his broad shoulders, "but, yes, I'm staying. I've closed on the house, but the sellers won't be out for another two weeks."

Which was when he was supposed to have returned from his honeymoon with Molly. *Oh, Molly, what were you thinking, to give up one of the few good men left?*

"Oh," she said with a teasing smile. "I understand. You'd

just like a backup babysitter, since you're going to be living in Cloverville now."

He didn't deny her allegation. "Buzz and TJ said that when Nick took them to the park this morning they ran into you. They said you read them a story."

"Yes."

"Like you read to the children at the hospital."

Even though pediatrics wasn't Josh's specialty, he knew what Colleen did. How was it that Nick had no idea? Because he didn't care. He was only after one thing. Not her body or her heart but her sister's whereabouts.

"So it's not going to matter what Molly says when she comes home?" she asked. "You're staying?"

He nodded. "It's not going to matter."

So Nick would be wasting his charm on Colleen. Even if she gave up Molly's whereabouts, nothing her sister said would convince Josh to forget about moving to Cloverville.

"Please," she said, "tell Brenna I stopped by."

"I'm sure she'll be down in a minute," Josh said, gesturing toward the pressed-tin ceiling.

"It's okay," she said. "I'll talk to her later." She didn't need Brenna to tell her what she already knew. To stay far, far away from Nick Jameson.

Chapter Six

Nick paced the grass around the blanket he'd spread out. The picnic basket anchored one corner of the plaid fleece while the breeze played with the other three. Tree branches swayed as the wind picked up, cooling the Sunday afternoon to such a degree that he found himself left alone in the park. No children playing. No dogs barking.

No Colleen.

No smiling-haughty-laughing-kissing Colleen.

He glanced at his watch. He'd waited almost an hour for her. More than thirty minutes ago he'd decided she wasn't coming. But still he waited. Because what if she showed and he was gone? Then he'd have missed seeing her.

And he wanted to see her more than he'd ever wanted to see anyone before. He swallowed hard. No, there'd been one person he wanted to see more than her. Bruce. He'd been too young to die. If only…

But could Nick have saved his brother from a broken heart? Hell, he wasn't all that sure he could save himself.

He pushed his hand through his hair. She wasn't coming. He was wasting his time. In the park and in Cloverville. He leaned over, reaching for the basket and the blanket.

"Are you always this impatient?" a soft voice asked.

The pressure on his chest eased, and he lifted his head. He'd seen her earlier, of course, in those short shorts and light cotton blouse, with her dark hair thick and loose around her bare shoulders, but still her beauty staggered him. His body tensed, and his breath shortened. How he wanted her. "Yes, I am impatient," he admitted.

"Then why'd you wait?"

"I don't know."

"Liar," she accused him, and her enormous eyes narrowed. "I don't think you ever *not* know what you're doing."

"I had to see you." It was that simple. He didn't care if she told him where her sister was. He'd only wanted to see her again.

"Liar." She repeated the accusation, in a breathy whisper this time. She'd been affected by his words despite her obvious resolve to not let him get to her.

His mouth curved into a grin as he observed, "You don't trust me."

"I was warned that you can be quite single-minded."

"Josh?"

She nodded.

He laughed, not surprised that Josh had taken it upon himself to warn her. Like Clayton McClintock, he had a thing about protecting others from pain. Too bad that his best friend wasn't as vigilant about protecting himself.

"You two have a pretty close friendship," she observed.

"A close and *honest* friendship." Josh had been right to warn her. Even though he wouldn't mean to, Nick would undoubtedly wind up hurting her. And probably he'd hurt himself, as well.

"So, be honest with me," she implored. "Tell me why you wanted me to come to this picnic."

"I don't think you're going to believe what I *say*," he said, reasoning with her and himself. She'd left him no choice. "So maybe you'll believe what I *do*."

As he stepped close to her, Colleen held her breath. Waiting. As he'd waited for her. She had watched him from behind the shrubs. She hadn't intended to come to the park at all, but she'd pretty well had to walk past on her way home from the Kellys'. So she'd snuck through the gates, and then she'd found where he'd set out the blanket and the basket—in the shadow of the broken statue. And she'd watched Nick, who'd exchanged his rumpled tux for faded jeans and a dark T-shirt, pace and stare at his watch. She hadn't intended to talk to him, but he'd waited so long.

For her. Josh was right—Nick was single-minded. She'd thought he was only concerned with finding her sister. But could he actually be interested in *her?*

He reached for her, his hands cupping her face. Then he leaned forward, his mouth so close she could almost taste his lips. But he touched her only with his hands. His thumbs stroked the line of her jaw while his fingers traced her cheekbones. "You're so beautiful."

She'd heard the compliment before, from men who wanted something from her. And Nick wanted something from her, too, she reminded herself. Although it probably wasn't to get her into bed, or he would have proposed a more private picnic spot than the park. However, the threat of a storm had stopped anyone else from coming to the park. The threat of heartache should have stopped *her.*

She shook her head, but his hands didn't slip from her face. "I'm not beautiful." Not like her sister or Abby or Brenna. She'd always been shaped more like a two-by-four than a woman.

His brow furrowed as he stared down at her. "Haven't you ever looked in a mirror? You're gorgeous." He sighed, and his breath teased her lips. "We already established you're not going to believe what I *say*."

So he *did*. Finally. He kissed her. His mouth hot and insistent, he deepened the kiss. His tongue slid over hers, teasing and tempting her.

Passion warmed Colleen's skin, flushing her face. She'd been kissed before, but she couldn't remember any man's lips but Nick's. He tasted like espresso, dark and dangerous and destined to make her heart skip beats.

"I'm seriously attracted to you, Colleen," he murmured against her lips. "I can't stop thinking about you."

But she reminded herself that he'd never noticed her until yesterday. Until the wedding-that-wasn't. She pulled away, and his hands fell back at his sides.

"I didn't come for that," she said, her voice shaky as she failed to summon the composure she'd sought. Maybe she needed the red dress and the confidence it had inspired in her.

"Why did you come, Colleen?"

"I wish I knew." She swallowed hard, then admitted, "I wish I were like you."

His brow furrowed in confusion. "How's that?"

"I wish I *always* knew what I was doing."

He narrowed his eyes. "You don't always know?"

Standing in the shadow of Colonel Clover's bent and broken body, she shook her head. "Not last night. Not when I kissed you. And definitely not now."

"Don't worry about it," he said. "Don't think. Just sit down and join me." He tugged her down onto the soft fleece blanket. "For lunch."

"It's too late for lunch." She hoped it wasn't too late for

her, that she hadn't already fallen for a man who'd never be able to love her.

"Then, dinner."

"It's too early for dinner."

"This is Cloverville," he pointed out. "Don't you roll up the sidewalks by four o'clock? Heck, what am I saying? There's nothing open now."

"It's Sunday," she reminded him. "Most of the town shuts down on Sunday."

"I see that," he said, gesturing around him. The swings, although empty, swayed. The merry-go-round creaked as it moved in the wind.

"It's supposed to rain." Mr. Meisner had told her the forecast that morning, warning of afternoon showers. While the wind blew and the sky darkened with clouds, not a drop fell. Nick's kiss, clinging yet to Colleen's lips, threatened more than the weather.

Nick shook his head. "Nope. I won't allow it to rain."

A smile at his arrogance teased her mouth. "So you control the weather?"

"I wish." He opened the basket and pulled out a bottle of wine.

"It's not the only thing you wish you could control," she mused.

"I'm not trying to control you," he insisted.

"No, you're not," she agreed. "You're trying to charm me." And that was far more dangerous.

He uncorked the bottle and filled a plastic glass with white wine. "How am I doing?"

She accepted the glass and sipped from the rim. "Mmm." The sauvignon blanc rolled over her tongue, crisp and fruity. "Wonderful."

"I'm doing better than I thought," he teased.

"I was talking about the wine," she explained.

His green eyes sparkled with mischief. "What about me?"

She sighed. "You'll know how you're doing."

"When?" he persisted as he poured himself some wine.

"When you get what you want." If he kept laying on the charm, she worried that he'd soon have what he wanted. For him, she would betray her sister and herself. But Molly had barely been gone a day, and she undoubtedly needed more time alone to sort out her feelings. She didn't need Nick pressuring her to talk to Josh before she was ready.

And Colleen didn't need her heart broken again—as it had broken when she lost her father.

Nick shook his head. "You're wrong about me."

Despite her worry, she laughed at his persistence. Josh might have understated his friend's persistence. "I doubt that."

"No, you're wrong," he insisted. "I don't always know what I'm doing. Or what I want."

Skeptically, she studied him over the rim of her plastic glass. "Really?"

He waved his free hand in a wide gesture. "I swear it's this place."

"The park?"

His voice thick with bitterness, he clarified his meaning. "Cloverville."

He reminded Colleen of Abby, when she'd been a headstrong teen determined to leave her hometown far behind her. Too bad she'd left Colleen behind, too.

"You don't like it here," she mused. She'd picked up on his contempt before but thought it had only to do with Josh being humiliated in front of the entire town.

He sighed. "No, I don't like it."

"Then what made you agree to open an office here?" she

asked, confused about why Nick Jameson, of all people, would consent to do something he didn't want to do.

"Josh wanted it."

Of course, friendship motivated his actions, like now, when he attempted to use her to get information for Josh—to find out where Molly was hiding.

His voice and eyes growing cold, he explained, "Josh wanted to move here because of your sister."

His resentment of Molly, obviously, rivaled his resentment for the town. Colleen could never date, let alone fall for, someone who didn't like her family. The McClintocks had been through too much, lost too much, when her father died; and Colleen couldn't lose her connection with any member of her family ever again.

Not calling Molly, not going over to Eric's and demanding to see her, to talk to her and make certain she was all right, was taking all her restraint. Maybe that was why she'd come to the park—she was weak from fighting. But Molly had asked for time, and Colleen had to respect her sister's wishes as much as she'd always respected her.

"I didn't know that Molly asked Josh to move here." Her older sister had been at college and then med school for so many years now, coming home only for short breaks, that Colleen hadn't known if Molly even considered Cloverville home anymore. Or if, like Abby, she intended to settle somewhere else. Her heart missed a beat at the thought of Molly living anywhere else. Her mother was right—they needed to persuade Abby to come home, too.

"She didn't ask him to move," Nick admitted as he pushed a hand through his golden hair. "Not outright. But she showed him the town."

"And he fell in love with Cloverville?"

"With *this* town." He shook his head. "I don't get it myself, but I think I understand his reasons. He wants a safe small community where he can raise the boys. I don't know if you noticed, but they're a handful."

She couldn't argue with him on that point, and she smiled. "But they're adorable."

"They're a handful."

"You were going to have them for two weeks by yourself," she reminded him.

His mouth curved into a grin and a dimple pierced his cheek. "Like I said earlier, I should really be thanking your sister."

"You should," she agreed. Although, after watching him with TJ and Buzz, she doubted he would have had any problems handling them. The way the boys had called him Uncle Nick implied he had a close relationship with them. She suspected he'd helped Josh with them a lot after their mother took off.

"So tell me where she is," Nick said, his eyes glinting flirtatiously, "and I will personally thank her."

She set down the glass on the blanket and rolled from her knees to her feet. "I knew that you were just after Molly's whereabouts."

He caught her hand and tugged her back down. "Come on, I was kidding."

She wanted to call him a liar again, but he'd just deny it. There was no point in arguing with him; there was no point in seeing him when she knew what he wanted had nothing to do with her.

"It doesn't matter, you know," she said.

"What?" Relief eased the pressure on Nick's chest as she settled back onto the blanket beside him. Not close, and she held her body stiffly as if unwilling to even brush against him, but she stayed.

"It doesn't matter what Molly says to Josh when she comes back. Whether they get married or not, he's staying in Cloverville."

Nick knew she was right. He'd been friends with Josh a long time. Once Josh gave his word, he wouldn't back out. He'd built an office. He'd bought a house. He wasn't leaving Cloverville.

But Nick could go. He could drive here to work every day. He didn't have to move to Cloverville, too. He could leave any time he wanted. But instead of leaving, he reached into the picnic basket and brought out all the little containers from the deli.

"Did you hear me?" she persisted. "It doesn't matter. Josh wants to live in Cloverville."

"I know," he conceded. He only wished his best friend was moving for the right reasons and not because he hoped he still had a chance with Molly. Were the McClintock women that enthralling, that no matter what they did a man couldn't get over them?

God, he hoped not. And not just because he was worried about Josh. He was worried about himself, too.

"You know he's staying?" Her dark eyes narrowed. "Then what are you…"

"I told you, Colleen. I don't always know what I'm doing."

But only since he'd met her. Before yesterday, he'd always known what he wanted and who he was—a bachelor, not just a man who intended to never marry but also to never give his heart. Because what if he did and he wound up like Josh or, worse yet, Bruce?

A sigh shuddered out along with her admission, "Then that makes two of us."

"Let's just eat, okay?" Not that he had an appetite for food. Only for her. For more of her sweet kisses.

"Let's not think. Let's just eat," he proposed as he turned his attention to the picnic basket, forcing himself to ignore the temptation of her mouth. "Which we could do a lot easier if we had spoons. I can't believe it," he murmured as he dug through the basket.

"No silverware?"

He'd thought the deli would have packed utensils in the basket, but apparently he should have checked. "No silverware. No plastic. Not even a spork."

"Spork?" she asked, with a giggle.

"You know, the cafeteria spoon with the teeth."

"Yeah, I know." Colleen ate in the hospital cafeteria on the days she volunteered.

"Don't tell TJ and Buzz," he implored her, "but we'll have to eat with our fingers."

She looked into the containers he'd set out on the blanket. "Well, most of this is finger food. Sandwich wedges. Fruit salad."

"Potato salad. That'll be a little messy."

She snapped the lid off and reached in for a chunk of potato, popped it into her mouth then licked the mayo off her fingers. "See, that wasn't bad at all."

He groaned. "No, that was all wrong."

"It was?"

He popped the lid off the fruit salad and pulled out a pineapple chunk. Then he held it to her mouth, the sweet juice running between her lips. "You're supposed to use *my* fingers."

"Oh."

He slipped the pineapple into her mouth, the fruit both tart and sweet against her tongue. She chewed but could barely swallow, her heart was beating so fast. She choked and coughed.

He wiped her mouth with a napkin. "Wrong pipe?"

She shook her head. "I can feed myself."

"Chicken."

"Hey, you don't even know me," she protested. The taunt was one she would have expected from her younger brother.

"No, chicken?" he asked, holding out a crispy strip of meat.

"Uh, yes." She reached for the morsel, but Nick pulled his hand back.

"No, let me," he insisted.

"I can feed myself," she repeated. His charm had already weakened her defenses. She should have left when her knees weren't shaking, when she'd still had some strength to resist him.

"Sure, you can feed yourself," he agreed reluctantly, "but that's not nearly as much fun as this."

He held the chicken in front of her mouth until she took a bite. She chewed and swallowed but leaned away when he lifted the food to her mouth again.

"No, I don't eat alone." Hand shaking slightly, she reached for the fruit salad and lifted a piece of cantaloupe to his lips. He sucked in the fruit, along with her fingers, running his tongue over her fingertips.

She shivered and not in reaction to the brisk breeze. "This isn't a good idea."

"No," he agreed, his voice hoarse and his eyes heated with desire, "but we're not thinking. Remember."

"I forgot."

He eased another piece of fruit into her mouth, a strawberry. When she bit into it, juice exploded over her tongue and dripped from the corner of her lips.

He leaned forward again, but instead of lifting the napkin to wipe juice, he pressed his lips to hers, kissing away the streaks of strawberry.

She pushed her hand against his chest, trying to shove him back. "No, we can't."

For so many reasons.

"Shh. We're not thinking. Just feel…"

And he kissed her again.

Colleen bunched his shirt in her hands and pulled him closer, her mouth devouring his as she had taken the fruit. Passion, long suppressed, raged to life inside, reminding her she wasn't a timid teenage girl anymore. She was a woman. With needs and wants.

And she'd wanted this man for so long.

"Colleen," he murmured her name as he pushed her back onto the blanket and followed her down, his body hard and hot against her as he covered her from chest to hip.

She welcomed his weight, wrapping her arms around his back as she cradled his body with her hips. But still she wanted him closer, her body throbbing with an insistent ache. The ache intensified with each sweep of his tongue between her lips. He slid it in and out of her mouth, teasing her.

She arched against him, pushing her breasts into the hard wall of his chest. His hands gripped her shoulders, holding her tight, but she squirmed beneath him, lifting her legs to cradle him.

Nick groaned, then skimmed his lips down her throat. His tongue lapped at her leaping pulse and his soft hair brushed her skin. She slid her hands up his back, muscles rippling beneath her touch, and threaded her fingers through his silky hair.

Recklessness surging through her veins, she didn't care where they were or who might see them. Nothing mattered but her desire for him. "Nick, touch me," she invited.

His hands moved, smoothing over her bare arms, brushing the slight curve of her hips to caress her lifted legs. His fingers traced the wings of the butterfly tattoo on her ankle. "This is detailed," he mused. "It must have hurt."

She shrugged. "I don't remember." It had been so long ago and so much had happened since she'd gotten it, losing her father, the strain on her family…

She drew him closer. It had been so long since she'd held someone, since she'd been held.

His body tensed and his erection pressed against her hip. "Colleen," he almost groaned her name, pressing his face into her hair. "I want you so much."

She moved her face so that her lips closed over his earlobe, then she nipped with her teeth. He shivered, and a sense of power surged inside *her*. He wanted her. He really wanted her. "Nick, I've never felt like this."

Her crush on Eric, her disastrous experience with the high school quarterback… Nothing had prepared her for these feelings, for the need burning inside her.

She shouldn't have come to the park, shouldn't have met Nick for this picnic. Because now her fantasies clashed with reality. What was a dream, and what was real?

Chapter Seven

Nick pulled back and turned his head, as if scanning the park. "*What* are we doing?"

"What…"

"We're in a public place." He rubbed a hand over his face and around to the back of his neck. "What are we *thinking?*"

"We're not supposed to be thinking," she reminded him. But she suspected she found that rule easier to obey than he did. Although she'd struggled to be careful the past several years, she'd still acted without thinking. More than once.

He rolled to his side, shifting his weight off her. "Did I hurt you?"

"What?" He'd barely touched her, certainly not as she'd wanted him to touch her. Maybe he couldn't bring himself to make that great a sacrifice for his friend.

He skimmed his hand up her side. "You're so…"

"Skinny?" Rory often taunted her that she was a rack of bones. It didn't matter how much she ate, she couldn't put on weight. She'd never have the generous curves of her friend Brenna.

A breath shuddered out of his lips as he shook his head. "No. You're delicate. Fine boned." His pale eyes gleamed in the faint light that was breaking through the blanket of thick, dark clouds. "You're beautiful."

Colleen's heart raced, and this time she accepted his compliment as sincere. The way he looked at her certainly made her feel beautiful. "Then why'd you stop?" she asked.

He lifted a hand and gestured. "We're in a public place. Anyone could walk up on us. In fact, I thought I saw something—a light—at the edge of the woods."

Colleen followed his gaze to the surrounding woods where tiny lights flickered. "Fireflies. Usually you can't see them during the day. But it's so overcast." She watched them flicker and sighed wistfully.

"What? Are you worried about the storm?" Nick asked, his gaze intent on her face now, the fireflies apparently forgotten. As he would forget her when he got what he wanted. Molly's whereabouts? Did he intend to drag her kicking and screaming to Josh? He had no idea how fiercely Eric would protect Molly.

If only she had someone to protect her.

"I'm not worried about the storm," Colleen assured him. Although the rain clouds lingered, not even a drop had fallen. "I'm worried about you."

"Colleen…"

"I'm like those fireflies, you know," she mused.

His brow furrowed, as if he struggled to follow what she was saying.

"Like no one sees them during the day, no one sees me," she explained. She'd felt that way when her dad was sick, invisible inside her own home. And in the shadow of her older, more beautiful sister, she'd always been invisible. "No one even sees me at night."

He shook his head. "I don't believe that."

"*I'm* not lying to *you*." Like he was to her.

"Then you're lying to yourself," he accused. "Because there's no way anyone could ever ignore you."

And yet he had. For years. She opened her mouth to point that out to him, but he kissed her first, his lips moving hot and hungrily against hers. "Your light shines all the time. I can't stop looking at you, Colleen."

But she wanted more from him than desire. She wanted love. His love.

Knowing she had to protect herself, she jumped to her feet and ran. But then her impulsiveness, like the passion she'd long suppressed, surged to life. And she turned and tossed out a challenge over her shoulder, "See if you can find me."

NICK COULDN'T REMEMBER THE last time he'd played hide-and-seek. Although Buzz and TJ often begged him to play, he never actually had to look for them. The twins always got impatient waiting and came out of their hiding places.

Nick doubted Colleen intended to come out of the woods. Something about the forlorn expression on her face when she'd compared herself to thosee fireflies compelled him to search. No one ever saw her?

Why would she think that?

He couldn't imagine that everyone—every man, at least, young, old and probably dead—didn't stare at her, as captivated by her as Nick was. But more than her beauty drew him. Her vulnerability touched something deep inside him, something no one else had ever touched.

His heart.

He groaned but not because briar branches caught at his jeans as he followed a path deep into the woods. He hurt for her. His fingers curled into fists at his sides. This was why he didn't want to fall in love—love brought only pain.

"Catch me if you can," she called, her voice husky as she threw out her challenge.

One Nick didn't know if he could, or should, accept. He felt *old*. Way too old and cynical for her youth and innocence. His feet stopped moving. He had no business chasing after her.

COLLEEN SLOWED HER MAD dash through the underbrush and listened. Earlier she'd heard him crashing through branches as he pursued her. Now she heard nothing. Only silence.

Had he stopped? Had he turned back and given up on her? Regret and embarrassment heated her face. She shouldn't have run. She should have known better; that no one had ever gone after her. But she'd thought he was different. And for a moment, on the blanket when he'd stared at her with such desire, she'd thought he was. That he really wanted *her*.

He'd even followed her. But only a short distance. He obviously wasn't used to having to chase women. They usually chased him, she expected.

The breeze picked up, blowing briskly. Her skin, bare except for shorts and a sleeveless blouse, chilled. In the distance thunder rumbled, reiterating the threat of a storm. She needed to stop playing games with Nick Jameson and go home—just like she eventually had every other time she'd run away. She edged away from the tree she leaned against and turned. Right into his arms.

"Gotchya!" His green eyes gleamed with victory. And something hot.

Colleen's skin warmed beneath his gaze and his touch. His hands cupped her shoulders, then slid down her arms, pulling her near.

"You're not very good at hiding," he admonished her.

She'd never had to be. No one had ever looked for her

before Nick. Overwhelmed by feelings both old and new, tears stung her eyes. She blinked them back.

"So, what's my prize for finding you?" he asked, that dimple of his denting his cheek as his grin widened.

"A prize?"

"You know. The winner always claims a prize," he explained. "How about a kiss?"

He didn't give her time to answer before his mouth claimed hers. Was the prize for him or for her? She felt like the winner as his lips caressed hers. A moan rose from her core, parting her lips. His tongue slid inside, tangling with hers.

She covered his hands with her own and thought of leading him deeper into the woods, where no one would interrupt them. Visions of the two of them lying together in the clearing, naked, teased her, tempted her. But the last time she'd given in to temptation, she'd been humiliated.

She tugged free of his arms. "You don't have me yet."

But she lied. Because he did already have her—in every way that mattered.

NICK STARED DOWN AT his arms, extended and empty now. She'd escaped him. Again. Instead of succumbing to frustration, he chuckled, feeling more alive than he ever remembered. "You better run," he shouted, "because when I catch you…"

What was he going to do? Never let her go?

His heart shifted, pressing against his lungs and stealing away his breath. He'd never wanted anyone forever before. But then he'd never wanted anyone the way he wanted Colleen.

"You can't catch me," she taunted. "You're too old and slow."

"Old?" he sputtered. "You think I'm old?"

To her, he probably was. Anyone over thirty was probably *old* to her.

"And slow," she reminded him, her voice coming from be-tween some branches to his left.

He followed, moving stealthily so that no twigs snapped beneath his feet and he could sneak up on her exactly as he had the last time he'd caught her, looking so pensive and lost as she'd turned away from the tree and into his arms.

He should have held her tighter. He shouldn't have let her slip away. When he edged through the brush, he stepped into the open, leaving the woods behind. Where had she gone? The park stretched before him, empty except for the blanket covered with their picnic.

Had she left him?

Thunder rumbled in the distance, farther off than before.

"Colleen!" he called, his voice becoming hoarse. He scanned the woods once again, catching the flicker of fireflies along the edge. Then behind him, near the crooked statue, he caught the slightest rustle of shrubs.

The bushes were overgrown there, probably to disguise the damage done to the town founder, and the branches were thick and high enough to hide one slim woman. He moved closer to the foliage, stepping over some flowers along the outer edge of the grass surrounding Colonel Clover. Then he reached through the shrubs. His hands closed over her bare shoulders. He held tight while he squeezed through the boughs and joined her at the base of the statue.

She winced in pain. Regret pressing on his chest, he loosened his grip. "I'm sorry. I didn't mean to hurt you."

"You didn't," she assured him. "It's just that one of the branches caught me."

He moved his hand and found an angry red scratch on her shoulder beneath his palm. He lowered his head and touched his mouth to the raw skin.

Her breath hissed from between clenched teeth.

"I'm sorry," he said a second time.

"You didn't hurt me."

Yet. The word hung between them, a thought they both shared. She obviously knew he couldn't give her what she deserved. Josh had warned her, but even so she'd come to the park. She'd joined Nick and she'd teased and played with him. It was an indication that she accepted the rules of their game. He moved his mouth from her shoulder to her throat.

Her pulse pounded against his lips, beating furiously in perfect sync with his. Just as they'd danced. As they'd walked. As they'd eaten. Just as they would make love. But they couldn't. Not here in a public park.

Not ever.

"You looked for me," she mused breathlessly.

He searched her face, her eyes, shadowed with lingering pain and soft with the vulnerability that reached deep inside him. "Colleen…"

He pulled her closer. Winding his arms around her, he wished he could absorb those old regrets and take them away from her forever. Her breath shuddered out, warming his throat. Then she pulled back and stared up at him, surprised, as if no one had ever tried to comfort her before.

"Nick…"

Tangling his hands in her thick hair, he pressed his mouth to hers and it opened for him. He slid his tongue between her lips, in and out. He took her with just his kiss. But it wasn't enough for either of them.

He had to touch her everywhere. He moved his hands over her body, over the soft skin of her bare arms, over the curve of her breasts. The nipples pressed through the cotton of her blouse, begging for more. His fingers shaking, he reached for the buttons. But damn, they were in the middle of the park. He couldn't see her as he wanted to see her. He couldn't touch her in the way he needed to touch her.

He curled his fingers into his palms, clenching them so that he wouldn't reach for her. So that he wouldn't tear her blouse open. But she pressed against him, as if anxious to be closer. He slid his hands to her hips and pulled her back. "Colleen…"

Her eyes dark with desire, she stared up at him. Her mouth swollen and moist from his kisses, she murmured his name.

His hands clenched her hips, pulling her against the erection straining painfully against the fly of his jeans. She tilted her hips, sliding against him. He cupped her bottom, lifting her, so her long, bare legs wrapped around his waist. And he groaned.

Dipping his head, he nuzzled his mouth against her breast, and through the cotton of her blouse and bra, he caught her nipple between his teeth. As he nipped, she moaned and arched her back, pressing closer. "Nick!"

He didn't care where they were, who they were. He wanted her more than he'd thought it was possible to want anyone. Staggered by the force of his desire, he reached out to steady himself, his hand closing around metal, old and rusted. Something creaked and groaned, then clunked heavily as it dropped to the ground at his feet. Colonel Clover's head, his hat dented and ear mangled, rolled across the toe of his shoe. "What the hell?"

He turned his attention upward, to the gray sky. "Was it lightning?" He felt as if, like the colonel, he'd been struck by something.

Colleen.

She wriggled out of his arms. "It wasn't lightning."

"What the hell was it?" Not love. He couldn't be in love

with her. No matter what he'd thought the night before, at the wedding… It must have been the moonlight or the punch. He couldn't be in love.

"The colonel often falls apart," she said. "The statue got broken a long time ago and nobody ever bothered to fix it correctly," she explained, her voice strained with emotions he doubted she'd share with him.

"I'm sorry, Colleen."

She bit her lip and nodded. "I know you didn't intend to take it that far."

The short hairs on the nape of his neck rose at the tone of her comment. "What didn't I intend to take that far?"

"I know what you're after, *Dr. Jameson,*" she said, her eyes dark with mistrust.

Her. But he had no right to her. He had nothing to give her.

"What do you think I'm after?" he asked, understanding she didn't believe he wanted her. Not really. How could such a beautiful woman have such low self-esteem?

"My sister's whereabouts. You want to bring Molly back, so she'll tell Josh to leave Cloverville and sell that office you have no intention of using."

Like her sister, she was smart, as well as beautiful. Admitting nothing, he reminded her, "You already told me I was wasting my time."

She nodded. "Josh isn't leaving. But like he warned me, you won't give up until you get what you want."

"This time he's wrong." Because he had to give up his feelings for her.

"You're giving up?" she asked, her eyes narrowed as she studied his face.

"I have to." He couldn't have what he really wanted. *Her.*

"I don't know if I believe you," she admitted, her lashes

blinking fast as if she was fighting tears. "You're really going to stop looking for Molly?"

He shook his head. He had a duty, as best man, to help the groom. He had to find the bride. "No."

Her breath audibly caught. "You're just going to stop using me to find her?"

He couldn't deny what had been his intention.

"Damn you," she cursed. Then she amended, "Damn me. I thought I was smarter now, that I wouldn't fall for a bunch of practiced lines."

"I wasn't lying to you," he insisted.

She shook her head. "Stop. Just stop. I'm not falling for…" She dragged in a breath. "Just leave my sister alone. The wedding was only yesterday."

"No, thanks to your sister there was *no* wedding."

"It's only been a day," she pointed out. "Molly will come home when she's ready."

"Josh deserves an explanation. She can't just stay away until she's *ready* to come home," he argued. "That's not fair."

"Sometimes life isn't fair," she said wearily.

Surely she was too young to know that already. But then he'd been young when he'd discovered that truth. "Colleen, I'm sorry."

"Just leave Molly alone," she said. "And leave me alone, too." She ran again.

And this time he didn't chase her. He only watched as she fled through the shrubs and then through the gates of the park. When he could see her no longer, he dropped his attention to the colonel's head.

Sighing, he squeezed the muscles at the back of his neck. The colonel wasn't the only one who'd lost his head. But Nick's heart wouldn't be beating so hard with fear and dread if that were all he'd lost. He'd come so close…not just to making love but to falling *in* love.

An emotion he'd vowed never to experience. Like the colonel, he'd been broken long ago. But what was broken in Nick couldn't be repaired by anyone. Not even Colleen.

Chapter Eight

Although the wind had died down, heavy clouds clung to the sky, bringing night on early. Colleen headed home, the fireflies lighting her way. Glancing at the illuminated dial of her watch, she realized that she'd missed dinner. But she wasn't hungry despite the little food she'd eaten with Nick. She wasn't particularly eager to face her family and their houseguests, either. Abby knew her far too well. She would realize that something had happened to Colleen.

She would know right away that Colleen had acted recklessly again. Colleen hadn't made love with Nick, but it didn't matter. She'd already fallen for him. Even knowing that he was only turning on the charm to find out where her sister was, she'd fallen.

Was she that starved for attention? That desperate? She'd thought herself so much older and wiser now.

She couldn't face herself right now, let alone look her best friend in the eye. Then, turning away from the house, she noticed a couple standing at the front of the white-sided Dutch Colonial house. The man's arms were wrapped tight around the woman and their lips met. Curious to see who else had fallen, Colleen crept closer, keeping to the shadows of the trees that lined the street and sidewalk.

They pulled apart, the man breathing hard. "Mary…"

Mary? Knowing she should look away, that she should give them their privacy, Colleen peered through the shrubs anyways. Her mother's name was Mary. That was her *mother* making out with some man at the front door of the house she'd shared with Colleen's father. The house where her husband had died, where she'd suffered from that loss for the past eight years.

"Wallace, I can't…"

Wallace Schipper? Her mother was kissing Colleen's old English teacher?

"I have guests," her mother murmured.

"Abby Hamilton's still here?"

Mary McClintock nodded. "We hope she'll stay."

Colleen seconded that wish.

"But even if Abby and Lara weren't here, Rory is," she pointed out.

Mr. Schipper snorted. "He knows."

She sighed. "Probably. But I haven't told him. I haven't told any of my children."

The pressure on Colleen's chest eased a bit. Her mother hadn't intentionally left her out.

"We're a little old to be sneaking around like this," her mother's boyfriend said, the frustration deepening his voice. "Mary, I want…"

"I realize," she said, "that *you* know what *you* want."

"But you don't know what *you* want." He sighed heavily, with resignation.

"I need more time."

Maybe that was all Nick needed, time to change his mind, time to give love and Colleen a chance. Maybe Josh was right and she was the woman who could get him to fall in love. And

Josh was right that Nick would fall hard. As a friend, he cared so deeply, was so loyal. As a lover, he'd be beyond any fantasy she'd ever had.

"It's been eight years, Mary."

Eight years since her husband had died, but still Mary McClintock mourned him. That was how much she'd loved him.

No, Nick was right about the pain that love could cause. Colleen didn't want him to change his mind and she wasn't changing hers.

Colleen crept from the bushes and made her way to the rear yard so that her mother and Mr. Schipper wouldn't notice she'd been eavesdropping. And then she stumbled onto another private moment in the backyard. *Another* man and woman stood close together, their voices raised in a heated discussion.

"I thought you were cool," Rory shouted. "I thought you wouldn't try to tell me what to do like everyone else around here does."

"Everyone else, or just Clayton?" Abby asked, her usually vibrant voice subdued as if she didn't want to make Rory angrier.

"Yeah, Clayton. He acts like my dad."

"No, he doesn't." Abby words echoed Colleen's thought. "Your dad was one of a kind. He was so…"

"I know." Bitterness filled the teenager's voice. "He was the greatest guy in the world. Everyone says so."

"Don't you remember?"

"Sure, I remember him," Rory said defensively. Then he continued, his voice thick with emotion, "But I was six years old. I don't have as many memories of him as the rest of you do."

Colleen's heart ached for her younger brother's understandable resentment. He'd been cheated. They all had.

"I'm sorry," Abby said as she placed her hand on Rory's shoulder.

He shrugged it off. "I don't want your pity."

"I'm sorry your dad died, but I don't feel sorry *for* you," she insisted. "You feel sorry enough for yourself."

"Hey!"

"I'm jealous of you. You had six years with a wonderful father, and that's more than I had." She swallowed hard. "Sure you lost your dad, but you still have all these great people who care about you. Your mom is so…" Abby's voice broke. "I'm jealous of your mom, too."

"I bet you're not jealous of Clayton," Rory quipped.

"No, I am. I've never had anyone who cared about me like he cares about his family. He gave up so much for all of you, for his father," she said, her voice rising in defense of the man who'd always given her such a hard time. "He was just a kid, himself."

"He was in his twenties."

"He was just a kid. He could have run off, like I did. But no, *he* stayed." Her throat moved as she swallowed hard. "He gave up whatever dreams he might have had in college."

"But he went to college, when dad was home sick. He took off…"

"Only because your dad insisted. And then he skipped all the parties, all the fun, and he came home every weekend to take care of things around here. To make sure all of you were okay."

Abby had always understood Clayton far better than he'd understood her, but part of that was Colleen's fault, for letting her take the blame for the colonel. Yet Clayton would have been the one least likely to believe the truth.

"How do you repay him for everything he gave up?" Abby asked. "You're spiking punch bowls and sneaking cigarettes in the backyard."

Rory. Regret twisted Colleen's heart. She'd been so busy working for Clayton and volunteering at the hospital that she hadn't paid enough attention to him—she should have tried to stop him from going down a bad road. She stood hidden, waiting out the rest of Abby's lecture. But then her friend left the teenager, with a hug and a playful rumpling of his curly dark hair, and headed back into the house.

Colleen waited until the pungent scent of cigarette smoke drifted toward her, then she stepped out to confront her brother. "You didn't listen at all," she said, gesturing toward his lit cigarette.

"Spare me, Col," Rory griped. "I don't need another lecture."

"No," she agreed. "Clayton lectures enough."

"Even Abby. And I thought she was cool," he said, snorting, then coughing with the smoke.

Colleen joined him on the patio, pulling the cigarette from his hand to drop it on the bricks and crush it beneath her heel. "So, you don't need another lecture," she said again. "You need your ass kicked."

A laugh sputtered out of him. "And you're going to do that?"

"No," she said, shaking her head. "You're still a tattletale. You'd run right to Mom. And since you're her baby, she'd take your side."

"So what are you going to do?" he challenged. "Tell Clayton?"

"What's the point?" She shrugged. "You obviously don't listen to him."

"Hey, he's gotta pay you to listen to him," Rory said.

Colleen's lips curved into a smile. "And I still don't always do it." Maybe she shouldn't ask Clayton for a raise.

Rory laughed.

"But I do better now than I used to," she insisted.

Like Abby, she'd come to respect her older brother for all

the responsibility he'd assumed when their father died. Still feeling guilty for thinking about running off when Clayton had done so much to support their family, Colleen had gone to work for him to help ease some of his burden. Unlike Clayton, she'd never wanted to join the insurance agency their father had begun. Yet she knew that Clayton had wanted to work *with* his father, not *in place* of him.

"C'mon, Col, you always do what you're supposed to," Rory scoffed, with disdain, not respect. "You work for Clayton. You volunteer at the hospital…"

"You know?" She had only told two people, Brenna and Abby, about her volunteer work. Molly had found out when she volunteered herself, and Eric, a paramedic, eventually had run into her in the hospital. She hadn't wanted anyone to make a big deal of it.

"I figured out you weren't reading the little kids' books for yourself," Rory said with another derisive snort. "Then Mom told me."

Mom knew. Of course, she did.

"Mom said I should be more like you," he muttered, reaching into his pocket for his pack of cigarettes.

Colleen grabbed the pack from his hand. "You're already too much like me."

His brow furrowed. "What are you talking about?"

Her breath shuddered out. "I've been selfish and irresponsible, too."

Rory laughed. "Yeah, right."

"You know why Abby left town?" she asked, wondering how much he remembered from that time when they'd lost their dad. In addition to losing her dad, Colleen had felt as if she'd lost her friends, too, since they'd all left Cloverville shortly after the funeral.

"*Left* town?" Rory scoffed. "Abby was pretty much run out of town for crashing into the colonel."

"She didn't do it."

"What?" Deeper furrows formed in his brow.

"I did it."

His eyes widened with shock. "You?"

"Yes," Colleen admitted with a heavy sigh. "And I let Abby take the blame."

"Col?"

She cringed. "I was selfish and irresponsible."

"You did that on purpose?" her brother asked. "You drove her car into the statue?"

Colleen shook her head. "I wasn't trying to hurt anyone." Not consciously, anyway. Maybe just herself. "But I stole Abby's car."

"Why?" Rory asked, aghast. "She was your friend. She would have loaned it to you."

"No, she wouldn't have." Abby had had plans for that car, which she was going to use to drive herself out of town after graduation. But because of Colleen she hadn't been able to graduate—she'd been expelled for malicious mischief. Abby had insisted to Colleen that she hadn't been passing, thanks to her ADD. "I didn't have my license. I was only fifteen, and I was running away."

"God, Col."

"I used to run away a lot," she admitted, her face heating with embarrassment as she recalled her stupidity.

"I didn't know."

"No one did."

His eyes darkened, and he shook his head. "No."

"I did," she insisted.

"Yeah, I *do* know," he explained. "I remember. You'd sneak

out with your backpack, with this look in your eyes." His own eyes glistened in the moonlight. "I used to be scared that you wouldn't come back, but you always did."

She nodded. "I never got far enough away to stay away. That's why I stole Abby's car. I was determined to go farther that time. And I intended to stay away." She sighed. "But the brakes failed and I ended up in the park."

"And ran into the colonel."

"Yes."

His breath hissed out. "It was a bad crash."

"I totaled Abby's car," she acknowledged. Her friend had had to take a bus when she'd finally left town. Colleen had insisted on paying for the ticket. In fact, she'd given Abby all of her savings. Abby, of course, had tried to pay her back, but Colleen had refused the money.

"You totaled the colonel, too."

She nodded. "Yes."

"I remember your bruises and cuts." His voice cracked. "You looked bad."

"I wasn't hurt that bad." Not physically. But emotionally something had broken inside her. She'd finally stopped being so self-involved, realizing she wasn't the only one hurting. "I never should have let Abby take the blame. But Dad was sick, and Abby didn't want me getting into trouble. I was such a mess back then. I was lucky I didn't get killed."

"And lucky that you had a friend like Abby."

"Yes, I could have been in real trouble for stealing her car, for driving without a license, for reckless driving. I could have really messed up my life." Her voice cracked as she said, "Instead I messed up Abby's."

"From what she's told me, it wasn't that great back then, but she turned her life around."

"Yes, she did."

"And you turned your life around, Col. You're like a saint now, or something."

She shook her head. "No, I just grew up. I had to. I lost everyone then. Dad died. Molly and Brenna left for college. Eric joined the Marines and Abby just left."

"And you blamed yourself," Rory said. The teenager was far more intuitive than Colleen had realized.

"It was *my* fault," she insisted. "I was so lost, such a mess. Like you are now."

"Hey."

"You can't argue with me. You're drinking. You're smoking. You're hanging out with the wrong kids. You're going to wind up in a crash like I did. But you might not live through it." She had been lucky that she had—as much for her family's sake as her own. They couldn't have handled two losses.

"Take Abby's advice, Rory," she instructed her brother. "Turn things around before it's too late."

In the glow of the back porch, Rory's face paled. "Gee, Col, dramatic much?"

A laugh sputtered from her lips. He could always manage a wisecrack, no matter how much he was affected. Maybe that was why no one had ever realized how hard he'd taken his father's death.

"And now you're spitting on me," he said, wiping a hand across his face, as if her laugh had showered him with saliva.

"Gotta do something to make you listen."

"I *heard* you," he replied solemnly, sincere for once.

She smiled and teased, "I guess there's a first time for everything."

"You never *talked* before, Col, not like this."

And maybe she hadn't. She'd been scared to open herself

up—even to her family. "Well, as far as I'm concerned, this conversation *never* happened." She narrowed her eyes and mimicked his tough attitude. "If you finally grow up and stop being such a little jerk, blame someone else." She swallowed hard. "Do what I did. Let Abby take the blame."

Clayton would love that. After banging his head against the wall of Rory's stubborn rebellion, it was Abby who finally got through to him. And maybe he'd finally realize how special Abby was. Apparently her mother wasn't the only matchmaker in the McClintock family.

"Sure, I'll blame Abby," he agreed. Then he reached out and did something he'd rarely done—he hugged her. "I don't care what you did when you were a kid, Col. You're still a saint."

"And you're still a smart-ass," she quipped as she patted his back and held him tight. When they pulled apart, both were blinking back tears.

"You coming inside?" he asked as he held open the door to the house.

She shook her head, needing a minute. "No, I think I'll stay outside for a while."

"Don't let Mom catch you smoking those cigarettes," he said, gesturing toward the pack she'd crushed in her hand.

She glanced down, and when she looked back up, he was gone. Inside the house. She settled on a lawn chair, tension easing from her body. She'd told Rory the truth.

Now, if she'd just tell herself…the truth about her feelings. How did she feel about Nick Jameson? Was it still just a crush, or was it something more? No matter what she'd thought earlier, it couldn't be love. She couldn't let it be love.

The screen rattled as the sliding door opened. "You're not getting these back," she warned her brother without turning around. "I don't care how big you are or how much you tattle to Mom, I can still take you."

"And I can still take you both," a feminine voice, rich with laughter, claimed. "Neither of you is too big to turn over my knee."

Colleen laughed as she hid the crumpled pack under her lounge chair. "Rory and I outgrew you before we reached our teens."

Only Molly was petite like their mom and had her big, generous heart. She'd probably agreed to marry Josh simply to nurture his motherless sons. Why had she backed out, then? Colleen wished she could talk to her and find out what had made her run. Had it really only been a day since Molly had disappeared from the bride's dressing room?

"You and your brother have quite a bit in common," Mary McClintock remarked. When she sat on the chair next to Colleen's, she leaned down and retrieved Rory's contraband. "I know what he's been up to."

"I never smoked."

"No. You never did."

But she'd done some other stupid things. And apparently her mother was aware of everything she'd done. Colleen tipped her head back and met her mother's gaze. "Mom?"

"I heard what you said to him."

Colleen closed her eyes. "You were eavesdropping."

"That's something you and I have in common."

Her face heated with embarrassment. "You saw me."

"Skulking in the bushes? You would not make a very good spy, honey." Her mother laughed. "Yes, I saw you."

And that was probably why she hadn't shared her feelings with Mr. Schipper. She hadn't wanted to share them with Colleen, too.

"I'm sorry, Mom."

Her mother's hand dropped onto her shoulder and squeezed. "No, I'm sorry."

"It's none of my business," Colleen said. "If you want to date again…"

"I'll date," her mother agreed, as if she had no intention of seeking her children's permission. Maybe Colleen hadn't overheard everything when she'd eavesdropped. "I wasn't talking about me. I'm sorry about you."

"Yeah. I am, too." Colleen sighed. "I should have told the truth eight years ago. Poor Abby."

"Abby would have left anyway. For eighteen years, she couldn't wait to leave Cloverville," Mary McClintock reminded her. "You just gave her an excuse. You can't blame yourself for her going."

Colleen shook her head, insistent. "I should have told the truth back then."

"No one would have listened to you."

Colleen nodded. "That's what Abby said. That no one would believe me."

"No, there's more to it than that. No one would have *heard* you."

Colleen winced.

"I *noticed,* Colleen." Her mother's voice cracked with the pain of the memory. "Like Rory, I knew when you took off with your backpack."

And still her mother had never looked for her?

"You would get this look on your face, as if you were trapped, and you'd take off by yourself for a while. I figured you just needed time alone. It's what your sister asked for, too, before leaving her groom at the altar. But you're not like Molly. You didn't really want time alone. You needed to know that you mattered." Her mother's voice was full of regret. "Now I know that I should have gone after you. I'm so sorry…"

Colleen stood up and pulled her mother into an embrace. "No, I'm sorry. Everyone was going through so much, and I was acting like a selfish brat wanting attention."

"You *should* have had my attention," Mom insisted.

"You were distraught. You were hurting as much as Dad was, knowing you were losing him." Colleen couldn't imagine the pain her mother had felt.

"You deserved to have my attention," her mother insisted. "You deserve so much, Colleen. You deserve a man who will love you."

"Mom!" Frustration sharpened Colleen's voice.

"I haven't seen you since this morning, so I don't know if that handsome Dr. Jameson found you in the park," Mary McClintock blithely continued. Despite what she claimed, she still didn't hear Colleen. "He stopped by this morning with those adorable twins, and he seemed really anxious to see you. He's so good with the boys."

"Yes, he is, but…"

"And he's so handsome," her mother continued. "He'd make some lucky girl a fine husband."

"How many times do I have to tell you that I don't want a husband?"

"I know. You're scared." Her mother sighed and admitted, "I'm scared, too."

Colleen blinked back tears of frustration. "Mom, is it worth it, to risk your heart?"

"I loved your father so much," her mother replied, her dark eyes glistening with unshed tears. "I had so many happy years with him. Wonderful memories."

"That ended in a nightmare."

Her mother shook her head but didn't deny it. "No. It's just that it ended before it should have."

As would Colleen's infatuation with Nick.

"I'm worried about you, honey," her mother continued. Her fingers touching Colleen's chin, she tipped her daughter's face toward the porch light. "You have that look again. That scared, trapped look, like you're about to run again."

But Colleen already had—from the park. And just as it had happened all those years ago, no one had chased her.

Chapter Nine

"So, Colleen, you'll type that application for insurance on Mr. Meisner's dog?" Clayton asked from where he lounged in the chair beside her desk.

"Sure," she murmured, distracted, as she stared at the screen of her desktop computer. The letters and numbers blurred together as her mind drifted back two days, to the park and Nick's kisses.

"I think a million is a fair amount of insurance on old Lolly, don't you?"

"Yes," she answered distractedly, then she mentally replayed their conversation and groaned. "You caught me."

"A million miles away."

Cloverville Park wasn't that far.

"You okay?" he asked, his eyes full of concern.

She nodded. "Yes."

"You're worried about Molly," he guessed.

"Not really. Molly's smart. She'll work everything out. She just needs time." Maybe that was all Colleen had needed years ago. Maybe she hadn't needed anyone to look for her; she'd only needed time alone to figure out what she'd wanted. She'd always gone home again.

"I'm worried about Molly," Clayton admitted, rattling her pens as he played with a container one of the kids from the hospital had made her out of an old soup can and a laminated comic strip. She'd always had a fondness for Garfield and little kids.

"You don't have to worry about her," Colleen assured him. "She's only been gone a couple of days."

His eyes narrowed. "So you do know where she is? You've talked to her?"

She shook her head. "No. Have you?"

"No." He sighed and leaned back in the chair again. "And that's probably a good thing."

"Why?"

He shrugged and looked at the ceiling. "My roommate."

"Nick?"

Her brother narrowed his eyes again, as if suspicious of her familiarity with the best man.

So she amended, "Dr. Jameson…he's still staying with you?" He hadn't given up when she'd refused to tell him Molly's probable whereabouts.

Clayton nodded. "He's worried about Josh."

"And he wants to find Molly for him." Despite his claim, he hadn't given up. To call him single-minded was to understate Nick's ruthless focus.

"Yes." His hand tightened around the pen holder. "And I think it'll be safer for Molly if he doesn't."

"He wouldn't hurt her," Colleen said, jumping to Nick's defense.

"Not physically," Clayton agreed. "But I don't think the doc has that great a bedside manner with people he actually likes. I can't imagine what he'd say if he found Molly, but I'm sure it's nothing she could handle hearing right now."

"I think he's more upset than Josh is," Colleen mused, remembering her conversation with the jilted groom.

"I think so, too." Her brother sighed. "I can't begrudge him his loyalty to his friend."

"But you want to protect Molly." Just as he'd tried to protect all of his siblings when he'd assumed his father's responsibilities. Only Colleen had gotten hurt on his "watch." She hated that he'd blamed Abby—and himself—for her foolish mistake.

"Has he been giving you a hard time?" Clayton asked.

"What?" Her pulse quickened, her face heating. "When?"

Clayton's eyes narrowed again, his suspicion regarding her attitude obviously increasing. "I heard you danced with him at the wedding. The reception. The…"

"Welcome-home party for Abby and Lara," she said.

He grimaced. "Yeah, that."

"I hope they're home to stay."

"You didn't answer my question," he reminded her, refusing to be sidetracked. He could be nearly as focused as Nick. "Has Dr. Jameson been giving you a hard time?"

Not needing her big brother to fight her battles, she shook her head. "No. He's just upset for Josh. He hates that Molly hurt him. They're really close."

His voice wistful, her brother asked, "Have you ever had a friend like that, Colleen?"

"Yes," she answered without hesitation. "Abby."

He snorted.

Had *he* ever had a close friend? Their father had been sick for so long that Clayton had never really had time to relax or just be himself. Their mother was right. He did need Abby in his life.

"Abby really is the best friend I ever—"

"I don't want to talk about Abby," he interrupted, his square jaw taut as he clenched it.

He never wanted to talk about Abby. He probably didn't even know about her business, which would make her a perfect tenant for the empty space next to the agency. "Clayton…"

"I don't have time, Colleen. I have two appointments in a row this afternoon. Mike Simpson's coming in to talk about life insurance."

"Again?"

"He's going to buy a policy eventually." Because Clayton never pressured. He was the kind of salesman their father had been, more concerned about the customer's needs than his own commission. "And after him, the Frazers are coming in to review their policies."

"I'll print out all their records for you."

He set her pen container back onto the corner of her desk. "I already did that last night."

Of course he had. Clayton did everything himself. Even though she was his office manager, he didn't really need her to run his office. No one had ever *really* needed Colleen. While she was afraid of falling in love with someone, she wouldn't mind someone falling for her. Adoring her. Hell, she'd settle for wanting—really wanting—*her.* Not her sister's whereabouts.

Clayton continued, "And I made notes on the copies."

"So you're all ready. I'll have Angela brew some fresh coffee," she said, referring to the agency receptionist. "I know Mr. Simpson likes it strong and sweet."

"Yeah, have her put on the coffee. Then run upstairs for that file," her boss instructed. "I left it—"

"Upstairs?" Where Nick was still staying.

"Yeah, I either left it on the coffee table or on the chest or the dresser in my bedroom. Yeah, it's probably in the bedroom." He brushed a hand through his dark hair. "God knows I'm not sleeping in there lately, so I might as well work."

She could identify with his sleeplessness, but she imagined her brother had another reason behind his insomnia. "Molly's fine," Colleen assured him. "You don't have to worry about her."

Clayton nodded then muttered, "It's not Molly keeping me awake."

"So what is?" She hoped he wasn't worried about her. Had Mom said anything to him?

"Uh, I really need that file. Mike Simpson is always early." He glanced at his watch. "And so are the Frazers. I won't have time to grab it myself."

Mike Simpson wasn't early. Ever. But apparently Clayton wanted some time alone before his appointment.

Colleen needed some time alone before she headed up the back stairs to her brother's apartment and her brother's house-guest. So she put on the pot of coffee herself. Then, knees trembling slightly, she climbed the steps.

Nerves danced in her stomach at the thought of seeing Nick again. But he was probably gone. Even though he was staying with Clayton, he had no reason to hang around the apartment all day. He'd taken vacation time to watch the boys, so he wasn't expected at the hospital. But that didn't mean he wouldn't show up to work.

Despite not having the bedside manner of his best friend, he was just as dedicated to his work. She could tell that he loved being a doctor; it was probably the only thing he'd ever loved. Even though she doubted he was in the apartment, Colleen knocked and then pressed her ear to the door to listen. Nothing moved inside; she heard no music or TV. She turned the knob and walked in.

For a bachelor, Clayton kept his place clean; everything in order, just as he liked his life. She searched the living room easily, but no file sat on the coffee table. Not even a paper or magazine had been left on the polished walnut surface. She headed down the hallway toward his bedroom in the back.

Sounds from inside the bathroom drew her to a stop outside the closed door. The pipes rattled and whined as water rushed through them. "Oh, no…"

Nick wasn't gone.

Before she could think to move, the shower cut off. Her pulse quickened at the realization that only a door separated her from a naked Nick. Then not even the door separated them as he pulled it open.

Water dripped from his wet hair, droplets falling onto his broad shoulders and trailing down the sculpted muscles of his chest and arms. Entranced, Colleen followed the trail of water down his chest and onto his washboard stomach, to where it stopped and was absorbed by the towel wrapped around his hips.

So he wasn't entirely naked. Just mostly. The towel reached only to midthigh, leaving his legs bare except for a dusting of golden hair.

"Change your mind?" Nick asked, his voice hoarse.

"What?"

"About running the other night. You don't want me to leave you alone." He reached out, his hands closing over shoulders. "Is that why you came up here?"

"I did…didn't…think…you'd be…" She averted her gaze to a spot on the bathroom wall behind his shoulder as steam from his shower and the scent of soap wrapped around them.

"You didn't come for me?" he asked teasingly.

She shook her head.

"Of course you didn't," he mockingly agreed. He was so damned arrogant. But then, he had reason to be.

She had to ignore those reasons. She had to ignore him. "I

came up to get a file for Clayton. He left it in his bedroom."
She gestured down the hall.

"So he's working at night," Nick mused of his host. "I
thought he had a woman on his mind, keeping him awake, too."

"Too?" She bit her lip too late. The question had already
slipped out.

"You know you're all I think about," he told her, pouring
on his charm. "I told you that at our picnic."

"But I didn't believe you then." And she shouldn't believe
him now. Even if dark circles rimmed his green eyes, verify-
ing his sleepless nights.

"It's true, Colleen," he said, his voice deep with frustration,
"Although I wish like hell it wasn't."

"I guess we have something in common after all."

"You think about me, too?"

She had for years, but she couldn't admit that without embarrassing herself more than she already had. So she shook
her head. "I wonder why you're wasting your time hanging
around Cloverville. Josh is fine, and your office isn't done yet.
You don't need to watch the boys."

"Like I said at our picnic, maybe I'm staying for you."

"You're wasting your time," she repeated.

"No, I'm not." He ran a hand through his hair. "Even
though I'm not babysitting, Josh is making use of me. I'm
working on his new house."

"I thought he didn't have possession for two weeks." Until
after his honeymoon. "He bought the Manning place, right?"
She'd canceled their home policy when they'd closed escrow.

He shrugged, and muscles rippled in his shoulders and
chest. "I don't know who he bought it from, but they moved
out early. And the place is a mess. We're peeling wallpaper
and painting."

She reached out to where green paint clumped a bit of his blond hair together. "You missed a spot."

"I don't see how. I turned the tub green. Your brother probably won't be too happy with me."

"Or me. I need to get that file for him." She needed to pull her hand and her attention from Nick Jameson first. But her fingers slid through his hair, ostensibly checking for more paint as she admired the texture of the silky wet strands.

"Did you find any more?" he asked, his voice hoarse as if he held his breath.

"What?" she asked, distracted by his proximity.

"Paint?"

"Oh." She pulled her hand away. "No. I didn't find any more."

He reached for her hands and lifted them, settling her palms against the bare, hard muscles of his chest. "You better keep looking."

His heart beat fast beneath her hand. Her fingers trembled against his skin. She wanted to touch. She wanted to taste. Now that she'd unleashed the impulsive nature she'd suppressed for so long, she couldn't control her urges. Her needs. She needed Nick Jameson.

IF NOT FOR THE WARMTH of her hands against his chest, Nick wouldn't have believed Colleen was real. She was only a figment of his overheated imagination, the one that had kept him awake the past two nights, taunting him with versions of what might have happened in the park, if Colonel Clover hadn't lost his head. If only Nick had lost his.

She curled her hands into fists, as if she intended to beat him. She already had; she just didn't know it. Nick couldn't tell her. He couldn't share his feelings with her because he doubted they were real.

How could he fall in love with a woman he didn't really know? He wasn't even sure exactly what she did for a living other than that she worked for her brother in the office below. Wearing a crisp white blouse and slim-fitting pinstriped navy skirt, she looked professional. She'd even bound her thick hair into some kind of knot at the base of her neck.

Nothing about her current appearance hinted at the existence of the passionate woman from the park. Maybe he had dreamed *her*, the woman who'd kissed him with such desire.

"You're getting a file for your brother," he reminded them both.

She nodded.

"Is that what you do for him?" he asked, curious to know everything about her. "Retrieve files?"

Her lips curved into a smile. "You make me sound like a dog."

He shook his head. "No one could ever compare you to a dog," he assured her.

"Maybe I am," she conceded. "Although my title is office manager, basically all I do for Clayton is fetch."

"He doesn't give you much responsibility?"

She lifted her slim shoulders in a shrug. "Like him, I took the state tests, and I have my insurance license in personal lines and life and health."

"Personal lines?"

"Auto and house insurance."

He nodded, as if he understood. But he knew little about insurance. His arrangement with Josh was that his friend would take care of the business end of their practice. Or they'd hire someone. Like Colleen.

No, he wouldn't be able to handle seeing her every day. It was bad enough that he'd have to drive in to Cloverville every day. He'd pretty much given up on changing Josh's mind about the location of their office. The boys loved the house their dad had bought. They loved the small town. And Nick was pretty sure they already loved Brenna Kelly, too. She'd been helping fix up Josh's new house, although Nick doubted she was in any big hurry to get rid of her houseguests.

Colleen's soft chuckle drew him from his thoughts. "I did it, bored you with insurance talk."

"You could never bore me," he insisted. "But I am tired." Of fighting his feelings for her.

"Josh must be working you hard at the new house."

He shook his head. "You're the reason I'm not sleeping. You keep me awake, thinking about you. About how sweet you taste, about how perfectly you fit in my arms."

Colleen closed her eyes and shivered. "Don't."

Don't tempt her to toss aside all her hard-fought-for caution and common sense.

"I can't fight how I feel about you, Colleen."

His fingers skimmed across her cheekbones to tangle themselves in her hair. The weight at the base of her neck eased as he freed her hair from the clip. Metal clattered across the floor, the barrette tossed aside.

She kept her eyes closed, steeling herself to resist his charms. To resist him. But he didn't play fair. His lips replaced his fingers, skimming across the curve of her cheek. He nipped at her earlobe, then flicked his tongue beneath it, against the hollow in her throat.

"You can't fight me, either," he insisted, his voice lowered to a whisper, a sensual threat.

"I'm not fighting you," she said, although she kept her hands curled into fists against his chest, holding him back. She fought herself, her own traitorous urges.

"Good, because you'd lose."

Her lips twitched into a smile at his arrogance. Not that he wasn't entitled to it. Most women probably weren't strong enough to resist him.

She wished she was.

His fingers touched her blouse, tugging at the buttons. She opened her eyes, shocked at his audacity. But she couldn't stop him. She couldn't wrap her hands around his wrists and pull his fingers from her buttons. She could only stand, trembling, while he undid every last one and opened the front of her blouse to reveal her simple bra. The thin white lace betrayed her, showing clearly her hardened nipples. He lowered his head and, through the lace, he closed his mouth around one, gently tugging and teasing.

Her knees weakened at the heat and sensation of his touch. And she stumbled back on her heels. Nick caught her, his arms sliding around her waist, then dropping to her hips. He lifted her and walked back a few short steps, bringing her into the bathroom. Steam warmed the room and heated her face.

He lifted her higher, settling her on the edge of the antique marble-topped vanity. Her skirt rode up, baring her legs. Nick moved closer, the terry cloth of his towel rough against her inner thighs. His hands, his clever healing hands, undid the front clasp of her bra, so that the flimsy garment fell away, baring her breasts to his hungry gaze. Then, his hungry mouth. His lips closed around her nipple once more, his tongue teasing the hard point while his fingers stroked her other breast.

She arched her hips toward the erection evident beneath his towel. He moved closer, pressing into the ache between her legs. Instead of easing, her need intensified. She dug her fingers into his shoulders, then slid them down the rippling muscles of his back, to his hips. She clutched him closer, and he groaned against her breast.

"Colleen, you're torturing me," he accused her. "Let me make love to you."

She opened her mouth to answer him, probably with an unequivocal yes, but then she heard another voice. Her brother's, through the intercom in the hall. "Colleen, did you find that file? The Frazers are early."

She slipped from the vanity, her legs trembling. "Oh, my God." She'd forgotten everything, her job, where they were, just as she had at the park. Nick brought out her recklessness. He wasn't good for her. "I have to get him that file now."

Nick nodded. "Why don't you bring him his file and then come back up here to me?"

She shook her head. "I can't. Clayton might want me to take notes," she lied.

"Who cares what your brother wants, Colleen? You're a big girl. Do what you want."

She closed her eyes and dragged in a deep breath. "I'm not a girl." Was that how he saw her? Young and immature, malleable? She'd done nothing to prove otherwise. Until now. "I'm a woman, one who knows better than to give in to a man like you, who only wants one thing."

"Colleen."

"You want to know where my sister is."

"I don't give a damn where your sister is!"

She almost believed him. But then she'd have to accept that he wanted her, only her. Not Molly. Not bragging rights. And that possibility opened her up to the risk of so much more than humiliation. "Then why don't you just leave Cloverville and me alone?"

"I'm afraid that I can't." With the resignation in his voice, the weariness in his eyes, his declaration appeared to unsettle him as much as it did her.

Chapter Ten

"You find what you want?"

The man's booming voice startled Nick into fumbling the paint cans. They dropped with a clatter and rolled across the scarred wood floor of the old hardware store. Josh had insisted that Nick buy the remodeling supplies here instead of at the big-box lumber store on the outskirts of town. Something about small-town loyalties or some such nonsense. He hadn't really been paying attention. Since meeting Colleen McClintock, he'd struggled to focus on anything else but her.

"Yeah, I found what I want," he assured the gray-haired shopkeeper. But he couldn't have it. He couldn't have *her*.

A gnarled finger precariously close to Nick's face, the old man pointed at him. "You're that guy. The one who's with the other fella, from the city…"

"What?"

"You were in the wedding-that-wasn't."

"I was in the wedding party," Nick admitted, thinking to himself that there'd been damn little to party about.

The shopkeeper shifted his hand away from Nick's face and snapped his fingers. "You're the best man. Sorry shame for your friend," he commiserated with a shake of his head, "being stood up like that."

"Yeah."

"That sure was a kicker, that McClintock girl taking off on your buddy like that." Despite the commiserating tone, his eyes twinkled with delight. "Word is she went out the window."

"Word is," Nick agreed as he retrieved the cans of paint.

Mr. Carpenter, according to the name tag on his tool apron, shook his head again. "That's just not like our Molly. She was always such a quiet, smart little girl, with her nose forever stuck in a book—unless she was running with that Hamilton girl." He chuckled. "Now, Abby, she'd go through a window. Whether it was open or not."

"Really?" No wonder Clayton McClintock was losing sleep over the blonde. She was like Nick, and she was not the type anyone should give his heart to because she couldn't be trusted with it. It was probably a good thing that Colleen didn't trust him.

The bell above the door jangled as another customer entered the shop. Afternoon sunshine streamed through the tall windows opening onto Main Street, illuminating all sorts of tools, paint, hardware and other odds and ends. Until the old fellow, whom Nick assumed was the owner, had cornered him, he'd been almost charmed by the place.

"Don't let me keep you," Nick said as Mr. Carpenter leaned around the tall shelf to peer toward the storefront. At the hospital, Nick always made a point of avoiding gossip—usually because he was the subject of it. He liked it even less when his best friend was feed for the gossip mill.

"That's fine." Mr. Carpenter waved off his concern. He lowered his booming voice to what he must have considered a whisper. "It's just that old busybody, Mrs. Hild—from down the street." Then, raising his voice so that the paint cans rattled and his hearing aid screeched, he shouted at her, "Rose, I'm back here with that doctor fella."

"Doctor?" she called back. "What doctor?"

"You know, one of the doctors building that office on the east side of town." He snorted his derision. "The doctors that make you pretty." Whispering now, he continued, "Ain't enough surgery in the world gonna help Rose with that one."

Nick nearly choked, stifling his laugh and remembering Josh's order not to alienate potential customers. When the older woman poked her head around the corner of the shelves, Nick was surprised that her neck was strong enough to hold it up—because of the hat she wore, its wide brim bedecked with flowers.

He nodded a greeting at the woman, then explained, "Josh is the plastic surgeon. But he doesn't do elective cosmetic procedures anymore." Not after his first wife, who'd left him once he'd made her beautiful on the outside. To Nick, she'd always be ugly on the inside, since she'd hurt his friend, just as Molly McClintock had. Another reason it was good that Colleen didn't trust him—he'd never forgive or accept her sister, even if Josh did.

"So what do you do, if you're not making people 'pretty'?" Mr. Carpenter pried, leaving Nick to conclude that he was really the bigger busybody.

Be friendly. Josh's command echoed in his ears. *We're going to be working in this town. I'm going to be living here. We want people to accept us.*

Nick eased the tension from his jaw and offered a tentative smile. "I'm an orthopedic surgeon."

The two older people gasped and their eyes widened, as if in awe. "Now that's what we need around here," the shop owner said. "Who cares about wrinkles?"

"Really, Josh specializes in burns and scars, but he's going to do more general medi—"

"My shoulder's so bad I can hardly wash my windows anymore," Mr. Carpenter griped. "Before he retired, Dr. Strover said he couldn't do a thing for me—that you can't fight old age."

Mrs. Hild's head full of flowers bobbed as she nodded. "Told me the same thing."

The old man pointed at the old woman. "Rose here can barely get up from her flower beds."

"Bad knees," the woman explained. "Not much can be done for that. I just wore 'em out."

"Actually, I can do a lot for both of you," Nick observed, mentally considering whether physical therapy, injections or surgery would be the best route to follow with these potential patients. He'd need their medical histories, of course. "As soon as the office is ready, I'd like you to make appointments."

"I wasn't sure about you guys, opening a fancy office on the other side of town—" Mr. Carpenter patted Nick's shoulder now "—but I think you're going to be a great addition to Cloverville, son."

Son. Only his father had ever called him son, and he'd stopped doing that after he'd lost his other son, his firstborn. But maybe that was for Nick's sake as much as his own—he hadn't wanted to remind either of them of their loss.

Mrs. Hild swiped at the storekeeper's arm. "You make it sound like he's one of the new shops. He's a *person,* Horace. What's your name?" she asked.

"Nick Jameson." He held out his hand, which she took into her surprisingly strong, callused one.

"Oh, you're one of those good-looking boys from the wedding party," she acknowledged.

"The best man," Mr. Carpenter said. "Before you came in,

we were talking about how unlike Molly McClintock it was to take off like that. It's more like something Abby Hamilton would have done."

Mrs. Hild's face creased in an affectionate smile. "Yes, it is. Molly's the last one of their group I'd have thought would do something like that. Now, her younger sister, Colleen…"

Colleen. Nick's pulse quickened at the mere mention of her name. He waited for the older woman to say more, but she just sighed.

Mr. Carpenter nodded.

"What about Colleen?" He had to know.

Mrs. Hild's eyes clouded. "Poor thing. She had the toughest time with her father's death. I often saw her disappearing with that backpack of hers."

Mr. Carpenter nodded. "She usually just wound up in the park."

Mrs. Hild continued the tag-team gossip. "She always went back home, though. Eventually."

"What are you saying—she used to run away?"

The older people nodded.

"And no one went looking for her?" Nick swallowed hard, struggling with his feelings. "She just went back home on her own?" An image sprang to his mind, of her slipping inside her house, her absence unnoticed, her beautiful face stained with all the tears she'd shed alone.

Mrs. Hild nodded again, then explained, "Mr. McClintock, God rest his soul, died at home."

"Slowly," Mr. Carpenter put in. "It was tough on the whole family."

"But Colleen was the most sensitive of all of them," Mrs. Hild insisted. "She took it the hardest. It had to have been awful for her, watching him die."

Nick's heart clenched as he understood Colleen's pain. He imagined her running off by herself, and facing the knowledge that no one was looking for her. No wonder she'd been so surprised when he'd caught her in the woods, if he'd been the first one ever to chase after her. But then he'd let her run away again.

"Poor girl," the older man said, his voice rough with sympathy.

Mrs. Hild sighed. "Yes, it would have made more sense for *her* to take off and leave a man at the altar." Her face grew pink. "Not that she would do something like that now. All that running, that was a long time ago."

And, yet she'd been carrying a backpack in the park the day he'd brought the twins there.

"She's a good girl," Mrs. Hild continued, "sweet and beautiful. She'd make some lucky man a fine wife."

Mr. Carpenter laughed. "You're getting as bad as Mary McClintock with the matchmaking, Rose. Give the guy a break."

"But he's moving here. He'll want to find a girlfriend," she insisted.

"He's a good-looking fellow," her friend defended Nick. "I'm sure he's already got a girl."

"No." Nick only managed to squeeze the single word into their back-and-forth conversation. Like a tennis match.

"See, he's single. And so's Colleen," Mrs. Hild volleyed back at the store owner. "He walked her down the aisle when the wedding party left the church. They looked lovely together. Him so blond and tall, and Colleen, so dark and delicate."

"No, I'm not moving here," Nick said.

"So the paint's for your office," Mr. Carpenter said, gesturing toward the cans. Nick's arms were beginning to ache from the strain of holding them.

"No. I'm picking them up for Josh."

"Josh?"

"The groom," he explained.

Mrs. Hild tsked and shook her head. "Poor man, having to raise those boys alone."

How did the town already know so much about them? Nick's doubts about opening an office in Cloverville returned. "He's doing fine. Really. He's working on the house he bought and he sent me for the paint. I really need to get back…" He gestured with the cans, but his companions blocked his way out.

"Whose place did he buy?" Mrs. Hild asked. "The Barber house?"

Nick shook his head.

"No, that wouldn't be big enough for a family," Mr. Carpenter said. "He probably bought the Manning place."

"That's it," Nick confirmed.

The shopkeeper whistled. "No wonder he's working on it. The Mannings never did much upkeep on the place."

"No."

"The Barber house is nicer," Mrs. Hild argued.

"Well, Josh already bought a house," Nick pointed out. Although he still struggled to understand his friend's determination to move to a town where he'd experienced such humiliation.

"Then, the Barber place is still for sale," the old woman persisted. "That would make a fine house for you. Not too big for one person, not too small for a couple."

Not that it was anyone's business other than his, but Nick found himself stating unequivocally, "I'm a bachelor. Now and forever."

No matter what he felt for Colleen McClintock, he didn't intend to act on those feelings. Ever.

"YOU SURE YOU GOT IT?" Clayton asked, his hand on the door.

"It's not my first time locking up," Colleen reminded him. "I lock up every Wednesday, and any other time you coach."

"But usually Angela's here, too."

"She's sick." Colleen suspected the receptionist mostly was sick of the two of them, rather than having a viral ailment, as she claimed. Neither Colleen nor Clayton had had the best temperaments since the wedding. Angela blamed the wedding-that-wasn't for both their bad moods. Colleen blamed Nick Jameson for hers. She suspected Abby was responsible for Clayton's edginess.

"So you're sure?"

"Yes," she said, "don't worry." She wasted her breath, knowing that worrying was all he usually did. "Get out of here. You don't want to be late." Clayton hated being late.

"Thanks, Col. You're the best."

At least someone thought so.

"After you close up, come down to the field and watch the game. Unless you have other plans…"

"No." No other plans. Except to avoid her older brother's houseguest. But if she asked if he'd invited Nick to the game, too, Clayton might get the wrong idea. Her mother's match-making was bad enough; she didn't need Mom enlisting Clayton's help.

"So you'll come?" he asked.

"You better get going," she said.

Before he could try any harder to persuade her to attend the soccer game, the phone rang. With a smile, she waved him off as she answered, "Good afternoon, McClintock Insurance Agency. How may I help you?"

The calls kept her busy until after closing. She forwarded the phone to voice mail, turned over the Closed sign and flipped the dead bolt lock on the front door. She could still get to the soccer field before play got underway. Clayton always left the office early on these days so that he had time to strategize with his team before the game.

But she couldn't take the chance that Nick might show up, too. She'd heard that he'd been seen around town, hanging out at Mr. Carpenter's hardware store and stopping by to admire Mrs. Hild's flowers, which flourished on the corner lot of Main Street. A soccer game could be his next stop, if he was trying to recruit patients. Athletes often broke bones or sprained joints.

The man had entirely messed up her life. She couldn't go to the hospital for fear he might show up at work, and she couldn't walk around Cloverville for fear she might run into him at home. "Damn him!"

"Your brother still treating you like a dog?" asked a male voice from the stairwell leading up to Clayton's apartment.

She lifted her head and met the eyes of the man who was really responsible for her bad mood. "No."

"So you're not mad at your brother?"

"No."

His mouth slid into a grin. "So you're mad at another man? Me?"

She shrugged. "I'm not sure if I'm mad at you, or just…"

"Frustrated?" He arched a blond eyebrow above one of those compelling pale eyes. "I could help you with that, Colleen. If you'd stop running away from me."

She bit her lip.

"But I heard that's *your* thing, running."

Her pulse quickened as nerves rushed through her. "Who've you been talking to?" Had her mother betrayed her?

Rory? Probably Rory. Maybe Nick had already taken in one of the teen's soccer practices.

"It's kind of common knowledge around town."

When her face paled, Nick regretted his admission. Obviously, she'd not realized anyone knew what she'd done all those years ago. He stepped out from the doorway to join her beside her desk. "Are you okay?"

She reached a slightly trembling hand toward her hair, pushing back a strand that had slipped from the knot at the back of her neck. "I didn't know."

"It's okay," he assured her. "Everyone loves you." Even him, he was afraid.

She blew out a breath that stirred the hair that hadn't stayed behind her ear. "Then they don't know everything."

He laughed. "I can't imagine anyone keeping secrets in this town."

"You'd be surprised."

He stepped closer and slid his hand along her cheek. "What's your secret, Colleen? The one no one knows?"

"Someone knows." She sighed. "Someone always knows."

"About the running away. Yes."

Her breath hitched. "They knew. All of them knew, but they never looked for me." She shook her head, tears shimmering in her eyes. "The whole town knew, but nobody ever tried talking to me."

"Sometimes it's easier to ignore a person's pain," he admitted, his throat thickening with emotion, "than to figure out how to talk to them and find the right words to make them feel better."

She blinked hard, but her eyes wouldn't focus. It was as if she faced her past instead of facing him. "I wouldn't have needed words. I would have just liked someone to look for me, someone to be with me, so that I wouldn't have felt so alone."

"I looked for you, Colleen," he reminded her. "I found you."

Irony tinged her laugh. "Now."

He narrowed his eyes to study her. She was in such an odd mood and she was obviously exhausted. There were dark circles running beneath the bottom fringe of her thick lashes. "What do you mean?"

"You've only noticed me now."

"I noticed you the minute you stepped out of the bride's dressing room at church. I'd never seen anyone as beautiful as you are."

She laughed harder, so hard that her dark eyes streamed tears. "Colleen?"

"You've seen me before, Nick." Her laughter faded, but the tears kept falling. "No, you didn't."

His emotions torn by her crying, he reached for her, closing his arms around her delicate frame. "I don't understand…"

"No, you don't. See. Me."

"Colleen, I can't take my eyes off you."

She wriggled loose from his embrace. "I've volunteered at the hospital for years, Nick, twice a week. I've seen you at least one of those days every week."

He dropped his arms to his sides. "What?"

Her voice shaking, she spelled out what he was unable to grasp. "You. Never. Saw. Me."

He rubbed his hands over his face. She was one of those girls, the volunteers who hung around the hospital hoping to catch a doctor. "I didn't know…"

Colleen's blood chilled at the expression on Nick's handsome face. He wasn't quite disgusted, but he was obviously disillusioned. "I'm not at the hospital for the reasons you think I am."

"No?" He sighed and pushed his hands through his hair now. "You're not like your sister?"

She shook her head. Molly hadn't been at the hospital for that reason, either. She'd been there because she intended to be a doctor. And she was smart and determined enough to get whatever she wanted. "No, but I wish I were like Molly."

"You wish that you would have gotten Josh to propose?" His voice deepened as if his throat was closing up. "Or me?"

She laughed, as she had earlier, with no humor only irony, at the horrified expression on his handsome face. "No. I've been hanging around the hospital for a while, Nick. I know you'll never propose. To anyone. Ever."

"You have me at a disadvantage, Colleen. You know me much better than I know you."

"Then let me tell you my deepest, darkest secret. The reason I do penance at the hospital."

"Penance?"

She sighed, disgusted with herself. "No. I thought it would be, but I find I get more from reading to the kids in the cancer ward than I give to them."

He shook his head, as if trying to clear it. "The pediatric cancer ward—that's a tough unit. Nurses don't last there for years, but you did?"

She nodded. "There are some volunteers who are there for reasons other than landing rich husbands, you know."

He laughed now, bitterly. "You couldn't prove it by me."

"Oh, poor, handsome doctor," she said with mock pity. "You have all the women chasing you."

He wiped a hand across his face again, his eyes gleaming with amusement despite himself. "My best friend met both his brides at the hospital where they volunteered."

"I don't know about his first wife, but I know my sister. She wasn't looking for a husband," Colleen insisted. She hated that she constantly had to defend Molly to him.

"I don't care what she was looking for. I want to know why you're there, why you're doing penance. Tell me your secret, Colleen."

"You've met the colonel."

He grimaced. "I know him. He's not a friend, or he wouldn't have interrupted what he did that day in the park."

"The colonel has a way of bringing you to your senses," she admitted. "He wasn't the only one who lost his head that day. I wasn't myself." She sighed. "Actually, I was. I was my *old* self. The impulsive, reckless self, who acts without thinking."

"Are you talking about running away when you were a kid?" he asked. "The way your dad died…"

"Cancer."

"That sounds like it was a tough situation," he acknowledged, his eyes soft with sympathy. "Anyone would have needed to get away from it for a while."

"No, my brother didn't. Molly didn't. My mom…" Her voice cracked as she remembered how strong her mother had been. "I acted like a selfish brat, running away when I should have been sticking with the rest of my family, supporting them. Instead, I stole my best friend's car and plowed it through the town park."

Nick's face paled. "Were you hurt?"

She shook her head. "Not really. Some cuts and bruises. Anyway, I got off easier than the colonel."

"You ran into the colonel?" he repeated, obviously stunned.

"Guilty." Confessing the truth lifted some of the weight from her shoulders. Telling Nick meant more to her than telling the truth to her younger brother. He meant that much to her. "But I let my friend take the blame."

"That doesn't sound like you."

"You don't know me," she reminded him. "Until the wedding, you never even noticed me."

Nick squeezed the back of his neck, as if trying to ease his tension. "Maybe I did. Maybe that's why it struck me so hard when I saw you, as if there was a connection between us. Maybe it was recognition."

"Recognition," she agreed. That was better than love at first sight. Safer. But all those years ago in the hospital, the first time she'd seen him, catching sight of him in the cafeteria… That had been when her crush began. Just a crush—not love.

"So I do know you," he pointed out, "and I think there's more to your story, to your letting someone else take the blame."

"Abby insisted," she admitted. "It was her car. She was known as a bad driver. She didn't think anyone would believe me, anyway." She laughed again. "Hell, my own mother admits that no one would have probably heard me. There was so much going on."

And that was why she'd run away.

Nick couldn't blame her, so why did she blame herself? "Why are you doing penance, then?"

In the roughest ward at the hospital. He remembered the gossips in the hardware store, how they'd shared with him that she was the most sensitive McClintock. How had she survived visiting that ward twice a week, seeing all those kids hurting? Dying, just like her dad had died.

He shook his head, awed by her strength. "Colleen, you're really…" An incredible woman. How had he never noticed her at the hospital? "When I heard about you running away, it haunted me—the image of your being all alone, crying, with no one to hold you."

She blinked hard, as if fighting tears. "That was a long time ago. I'm fine," she insisted. "I don't need your pity."

"I don't pity you," he insisted. "I understand you, though."

She shook her head, as if she doubted him or thought he

was feeding her another line, making another play in their little game of cat and mouse.

"Come upstairs with me, Colleen," he said.

She shook her head again. "No, that's not a good idea. Not now." Not when she was most vulnerable, he understood that, but he was vulnerable, too, right now. To think that she had almost done…what Bruce had done.

"I just want to talk," he insisted. "I want to tell you something."

She'd shared her deepest, darkest secret. It was time he shared his.

Chapter Eleven

He dragged in a deep breath, bracing himself to reveal something only a few people he trusted implicitly knew. And he hadn't had to tell them. They'd been there.

He turned toward where she sat on the leather couch in her brother's sun-drenched living room and said, "I understand feeling guilty for stuff in your past, for stuff you did or didn't do."

She shook her head. "Doctors can't blame themselves for losing patients, Nick. I've been around the hospital long enough to know that no doctor—not even you—is God. You can't save everyone."

"I couldn't save my brother." He'd said the words with such force that they seemed to echo eerily through Clayton's apartment.

"What?"

"It wouldn't have even taken that much. I didn't need to be a surgeon yet, then, to know he'd been hurting." He dragged his hand over his face, wishing he could wipe away the past. "His wife took off on him, but not before she told him that she'd been sleeping around their entire marriage. She even claimed that the baby she was carrying wasn't his.

She'd been his whole world, he'd loved her so much. More than life itself."

Colleen's breath hitched. "He killed himself?"

Nick nodded. "Not quick and clean. But slowly—bit by bit until there was nothing left of him." His breath shuddered out. "And because it was slow, I could have stopped him. I could have saved him. But I did nothing."

He hadn't wanted to admit that his big brother—his idol— hadn't been infallible. Josh had tried to point out to him that Bruce was in trouble, that someone had to help him before he drank himself to death. Nick hadn't wanted to listen, hadn't wanted to believe that his brother needed help.

"How old were you?" she asked, her voice tender.

"Seventeen." He'd been pretty screwed up for a while afterward.

"Nick, you were just a kid."

But Bruce had been just a kid—even younger—when he'd saved Nick.

"You were just a kid when you ran away," he pointed out. "You didn't let that absolve you of guilt."

"I blame myself for *my* actions, for what *I* did. Not for what someone else did."

"I'm blaming myself for my *lack* of action, for doing *nothing* to stop my brother from killing himself." He hadn't talked about Bruce in so long that the emotions came rushing up, choking him, but he managed to add, "No one died over what you did."

But she could have died. The thought crept into his mind, scaring him. "Did you…did you do it on purpose?"

"Hit the colonel?" she asked. "No. Abby's car had bad brakes, and I hadn't even taken drivers' training yet."

"So give yourself a break, okay?" he ordered her.

Her eyes, so big and soft, filled with tears again. "I have—

really," she insisted. "You're the one who has to give himself the break."

"Colleen…"

"How'd he do it?" she asked.

"Slowly, with the bottle, drinking himself into oblivion. And then he got behind the wheel of his car one night and crashed into a tree."

"He was drunk. It was an accident." Her voice was insistent. "Like when I hit the colonel."

"That's the funny thing," he said, although he could find nothing humorous about his brother's death. "That one night he hadn't been drinking. He'd been perfectly sober when he crashed into that tree."

"Nick…"

"He was still alive when the police got there. Still alive when the paramedics got him to the hospital. They lost him in the E.R., in trauma."

"That's why you became a doctor," she said. "Because even though you hadn't been able to save him, you might be able to save someone else."

Nick shook his head. For years Josh had tried to convince him to let himself off the hook, but he couldn't. "I wouldn't have had to be a doctor to save Bruce. I only had to be his brother, his friend, but I let him down. I left him alone when he needed me most." The only time Bruce had ever needed him, and his little brother had failed him.

"That's why you're pushing so hard to find out where Molly is," she said. "You're worried that you'll lose Josh the way you lost your brother."

He nodded.

"You won't," she insisted. "Josh isn't like that."

"My brother was the strongest man I knew." He shared with

her more than he'd ever shared with anyone—even those few people who'd been there. "My hero."

"How much older than you was he?"

"Ten years."

"He wouldn't have listened to you," Colleen said. "I know how it is to be a younger sibling, trying to talk to older siblings. He wouldn't have listened to you—no matter what you said—what you tried."

Nick sighed, and the pressure that had always been there on his chest, for fifteen years, began to ease. "You're probably right."

"I know I'm right." Colleen stood up and closed the short distance between them. Then she wrapped her arms tight around his broad shoulders, shoulders that had carried an unnecessary burden for far too long. She wanted to offer the comfort she instinctively knew he'd never accepted from anyone. Because he'd been too consumed with guilt over how he'd failed his brother, he'd failed himself, as well.

He cupped her head, lifting her knot of hair slightly so that the tension in her neck eased. "I don't want your pity, Colleen." His other arm wrapped around her back, clasping her tight to the hard length of his body. "I just want *you*."

"Then take me," she offered.

"I won't be able to stop this time—no matter who walks in or whose head falls off."

"As long as it's not yours and we lock the door, we should be good," she said, stepping back toward the hall. "Clayton won't be home for hours."

Despite her flirtatious words and willing acquiescence, Colleen recognized the risk she was taking. She was giving her heart to a man who hadn't asked for it; he only wanted her body. Whether he was ready or not, he was going to get both.

He lifted her and carried her the few short steps down the hall to the guest bedroom, setting her down only so that he could close and lock the door. "Done."

"It's nice to know someone listens to me," she mused.

"I'm listening, Colleen," he promised. "Tell me what you want."

His heart. But that would be asking for too much. "You."

He pulled his T-shirt, which was spattered with paint, over his head and tossed it onto the gleaming hardwood floor. Then he undid the snap of his jeans. The teeth of the zipper rasped as he dragged down the tab. He pushed the denim down his legs, along with his knit briefs, dropping them onto the floor at his feet, so that he stood naked—gloriously naked—before her.

Suddenly she was too hot in her silk blouse and linen skirt. Her skin burned, and her mouth grew dry as she stared at him. His heavily muscled chest, ripped abs and those long, golden-hair-dusted legs. He was too much. Especially the long, hard length of his erection.

"You're flushed," he observed, stepping closer and pressing a hand against her forehead. "Do you have a fever?"

She shook her head. "I don't want to play doctor. I don't want to play any games at all."

"Colleen," he murmured, his voice thick with emotion.

Already, they'd shared so much—more than Colleen had ever shared with anyone. And now she wanted to share more. Her body. She reached for the buttons of her blouse, her hands amazingly steady as she edged the mother-of-pearl clear of the silk. When the buttons were undone, she tugged the garment from her waistband and shrugged it off so that it joined his clothes on the floor. She eased the hook free of the clasp on her skirt, and the linen joined the silk, leaving her covered only by two scraps of lace.

Nick's breath shuddered out. He was awed, as always, by her beauty. But he kept his hands clenched at his sides and touched her only with his lips, his mouth brushing across hers in a featherlight caress.

She moaned, parting her lips for his possession. He deepened the kiss, sliding his tongue in and out of her mouth. Her fingers tangled in his hair, pulling him closer, but it still wasn't enough.

He backed her toward the bed until her knees connected with the mattress and she tumbled onto the soft cotton sheets. She lifted her arms, reaching for him. But he stood above her, staring down at her long, graceful legs and her lean torso.

Only those bits of lace kept him from seeing all of her. He reached down and undid the front clasp of her bra. She eased up and pulled the straps from her arms. Leaning back on her elbows, she lifted her legs—those long, sexy-as-hell, bare legs.

"Colleen…" he groaned as his body pulsed, demanding he take her quickly, insisting that he make her his.

But she deserved more. She deserved someone who wasn't afraid to offer her everything—including his heart. The thought of her with any man other than him had his fist clenching harder as jealousy gripped him. She was his.

Not forever. He didn't trust forever. But for this stolen moment of time, she would be his. He wanted to savor every minute, every inch of her silky skin—every taste of her sweet mouth.

Bracing his hands beside her head, he leaned over and once again just brushed his mouth across hers.

Colleen wanted more than kisses. She'd waited so long for someone she cared about to notice her, and now she wanted it all. She reached for him, digging her nails into his shoulders, pulling him down onto her.

His erection throbbed against her hip. She knew he wanted

more, too. But he caught her hands and held them above her head. "Let me take my time."

And he did. Kissing her cheek, her chin, her throat, every inch of her shoulders. He even nibbled along the ridge of her collarbone. Colleen squirmed on the bed, loving every sensation but wanting more.

He gave her more.

His mouth closed around one nipple while his hand stroked the other, then lower, over her quivering abdomen to the edge of her panties. He teased her with his mouth and his fingers until her body tensed, and then she shuddered and screamed his name, "Nick!"

"You're so easy…"

"Easy!" She flashed back to high school, to the things said about her after she'd given her virginity to the quarterback. "How dare…"

"Shh," he murmured against her lips as he kissed her again. "You're easy to please. You make me feel…"

Things he'd never felt before. Like love. But he wouldn't admit that to her. He couldn't say the words, but he could show her. He worshipped her with his hands and his mouth, making her sob with pleasure. Then, when he could put off his own desires no longer, he reached for a condom, sheathed himself and slid into her wet heat.

Her muscles resisted; she was so tight. "Colleen…"

"It's been a long time," she admitted. But she wrapped her legs around his waist, not letting him pull away. Her hips arched, taking him deeper.

He stared into her face, which flushed with pleasure as he started to move again. Slowly. She was hot. "How long?"

She shifted beneath him and murmured, "A while. You're so big, so deep…"

He thrust deeper, and she cried out. But not with pain. Her pleasure poured over him. He thrust again and again, gently, but with passion until she dug her nails into his back and shouted his name. Then he let himself go, burying himself deep inside her as he came.

"Colleen!" Unwilling to leave her, he rolled over so that she lay across his chest, her body limp and spent.

"Wow," she murmured. "I think I understand why all the women chase you. I never paid much attention before, but now I know…"

How had he never paid any attention to her? She'd been so close to him, twice a week, and he'd never noticed her. His arms wound tight around her, unwilling to believe he'd been so ignorant.

Or maybe he'd been smart to ignore her, rather than doing what they'd just done. "Colleen, why has it been so long for you?"

She lifted her bare shoulders in a slight shrug.

"Did you get your heart broken?"

Teeth nibbling her bottom lip, she shook her head. "No. My pride but not my heart. Once, I was stupid enough to let some guy use me, and I never intended to do that again."

"I'm not using you, Colleen," he insisted.

"You're not offering me marriage and babies, either," she observed.

Was that what she wanted?

"It's okay," she assured him with a quick laugh. "I understand that you won't let yourself believe that every woman isn't like your sister-in-law or Josh's ex." She obviously knew him well. "You'll never trust a woman enough to love her. I know that."

It wasn't that he mistrusted every woman. He simply didn't

trust himself not to fall for the wrong one, as Bruce and Josh had done. "Then why…"

"Because I *could* love you."

His heart, still beating hard from making love, raced into overdrive. "Colleen…"

She pressed her fingers against his lips again. "Don't worry. I don't. I know you don't want that." She sighed. "I can't blame you. I don't want to love anyone, either."

"Because of some stupid ass?" Whom he wanted to beat up for hurting her.

"No. He has nothing to do with my reasons."

"Because of your dad?" he realized.

She nodded. "My mom was destroyed when he died. We lost both of them for a while. But she's fought back. Hell, she's even dating again. She's a stronger woman than I am, though. I wouldn't survive a loss like hers."

"You're stronger than you give yourself credit for being."

NICK'S WORDS RANG IN her mind. She hoped he was right. That she was stronger than she thought. She would need to be to get over him. Despite what she'd told him, it was too late. She couldn't make herself not love him because she hadn't been aware of when she'd begun to love him. Before the wedding? Had she had more than a crush on the dashing Dr. Jameson?

And now, having gotten to know him so well, both intimately and emotionally, she loved him more. When would she stop acting so recklessly? How could she have fallen for anyone, let alone a man who wanted nothing to do with love?

The kitchen door slammed open, startling her where she sat on a stool at the center island. Masking her extreme emotions, she turned toward the woman who'd just walked in dripping water on the tiled floor.

"How'd you get all wet?" she asked Abby Hamilton, whose blond hair was sodden, as were her tank top and shorts. "There's not a cloud in the sky."

Only in her heart.

"Oh, there is," Abby assured her. "There's been a dark cloud hanging over my head since the minute I came back to Cloverville."

Colleen laughed, with real amusement this time, and she remembered why she wanted Abby to move back home. She stood up so she wouldn't fall off her stool. "How very Eeyore of you. You've been watching too many *Winnie-the-Pooh* videos with Lara."

"You know that black cloud," Abby insisted as she helped herself to a Popsicle from the freezer. "You call it Clayton."

Colleen laughed again. "Clayton, a black cloud? The description fits him pretty well." Her laughter faded as she realized who else the description fit. Nick. Ever since his arrival in town, he'd stormed her emotions, her heart.

"Where've you been?" Abby asked her. "I've hardly seen you at all the past few days, and you live here."

A few days? Was that all it had been—all it had taken for everything to change forever for her? Her face heated as she thought of what she'd done with Nick. "I…I…"

Abby's blue eyes narrowed. And Colleen thought about why she'd been avoiding her friend the past few days despite her promise to her mom that she'd help convince Abby to move home. She resisted the urge to squirm under Abby's scrutiny and instead leaned back against the counter, as if she were carefree. Something she'd never really been, except for that one wonderful day when their entire group of friends had gone into Grand Rapids and gotten tattoos. Well, everyone but Abby. Clayton, working on a tip from Rory, had tracked them down before Abby had been able to get hers. And it had been her idea.

"Colleen, what have you been up to?" Abby persisted, her blue eyes narrowed with suspicion.

More like whom. She stammered, "N-nothing."

"You've talked to Molly!" Abby accused, pointing the Popsicle at her as if it were a weapon. "She's fine and there's no reason for me to stay here any longer. You're all just conspiring to keep me here."

That had been the plan. But Colleen had been distracted—because of Nick. Her skin chilled as if Abby had pressed the frozen treat against her face instead of holding it a foot away. "I swear I haven't talked to Molly." She sighed. "I wish I could, though."

She needed her big sister right now—she needed a shoulder to cry on and she didn't want to distract Abby from Clayton. From the way her brother had been acting, Colleen suspected that he'd not be able to fight his feelings for Abby much longer.

Abby wasn't too preoccupied with Clayton to notice Colleen's unhappiness, however. "Are you *okay?*" she asked.

"Of course. I'm fine." She fought to steady her voice. "I understand Molly being confused and needing time to think."

Abby sighed. "Yeah, so do I."

For the first time since she was fifteen years old, Colleen was tempted to run away again.

Chapter Twelve

Nick rolled the paint onto the wall, and the green that Brenna had chosen for the kitchen blurred before his eyes. He saw only Colleen, naked in his arms, her face flushed with passion as he brought her pleasure. She'd brought him pleasure, too—ecstasy he'd never known before.

And never intended to experience again. He couldn't risk it. He'd already fallen for her, and if he fell any deeper he might fool himself into thinking she could fall for him, too. That she could love him, not just now but *forever.*

And forever wasn't possible. For one thing, she was too young. She'd change her mind about him, grow bored staying at home alone while he worked long hours—like his sister-in-law had grown bored, and Josh's first wife. Even with the shorter hours of private practice, he'd be busy, preoccupied with patients or the past. He didn't have enough to offer her, to keep her.

Something wet and thick splattered his face, and he turned his attention to the roller. But the foam had dried out since he hadn't bothered to dip it in the pan of paint again. More paint drops splattered his face and slid down his neck. "Hey, Buzz. I'm going to get you for that."

Buzz had been giving Nick the hardest time during their various remodeling projects and he was responsible for most of the paint Nick had had to scrub off his body and out of his hair. Before turning away from the wall, he warned the little boy, "You better run."

He whirled around, ready to chase down the wild little boy, but neither of the twins stood behind him. Only Josh, a dripping paintbrush in his hand, occupied the kitchen.

"Where are the boys?" Nick asked.

Josh's eyes twinkled with amusement. "Brenna took them back to her house for naps."

"Naps?" They slept? He would have to see it to believe it.

"Working on the house tires them out," Josh explained.

They weren't the only ones. But Nick probably wouldn't be that tired if he could manage to sleep at night. He couldn't, however—not with thoughts of Colleen taunting him. It hadn't even been a week since the wedding, but he was more exhausted now than he'd been during his internship, when he'd worked and studied weeks on end with almost no rest.

"I didn't see them leave." How had he not noticed the absence of their endless chatter and boundless energy?

"You haven't been very aware of anything today," Josh accused him. "I've been calling your name for a while now."

He shrugged. "I often ignore you, so that's nothing different."

"You are," Josh insisted. "You've been different since the wedding."

"The wedding-that-wasn't."

Instead of being annoyed, as Nick was over everyone calling it that, Josh laughed. "You're not going to distract me."

"Probably not," Nick readily agreed. "I don't have red hair and big…"

More paint splattered his face from Josh's dripping paintbrush. Nick blinked and wiped at his eyes and mouth, unable to finish his description of Brenna Kelly. But his best friend knew what she looked like—Nick had caught him staring at her often enough.

Righteous anger flashed through Josh's eyes and tightened the line of his jaw. "Damn you!"

Nick laughed. "See, I distracted you. Or was that her…"

"Who's distracting you?" Josh asked. "Or do I need to ask? Let me see. She has brown hair and big brown eyes."

Hair the color of sable. Eyes the color of milk chocolate.

"And an innocence and vulnerability about her that suggests she'd be easily hurt." Josh set his paintbrush weapon onto the plastic-covered counter. "Are you going to hurt her?"

"You didn't marry her sister," Nick reminded him. "You're not her big brother."

The same righteous anger Josh had shown for Brenna flashed through his eyes again, as he defended himself. "I'm her friend."

"You've only just met her."

Josh shook his head, his dark hair totally paint free. "I've known Colleen for years."

"You have?" How had he not known this? How had *he* not known her or at least noticed her?

"From the hospital."

"You knew she volunteered?"

"You didn't?" Josh laughed. "Oh, that's right. You make it a point to never pay attention to the volunteers or the staff. Only the patients."

"It's kept my life uncomplicated," Nick pointed out. Then because they'd never pulled their punches, either literally or figuratively, he added, "Your life would have been better if you'd done the same."

"Easier, maybe," Josh agreed. His chin lifted with pride, he defensively added, "But not better. I don't regret having my sons."

"They're good kids." Despite their penchant for flushing things down the toilet and flinging paint. But apparently they'd gotten that last bad habit from their father.

Josh laughed. "I thought we'd sworn we would never lie to each other."

"No, really they are," Nick insisted. He hadn't realized it until they'd moved to Cloverville, though. The town, and Brenna Kelly, had been good for them.

Josh grinned, his eyes shining with a father's pride. "Yes, they are."

Nick glanced around the half-painted kitchen—Josh's half, not his. The other rooms in the sprawling brick ranch house were finished. They'd tackled the kitchen last because Josh figured he'd use a take-out menu more than the oven or stove. "The house is finally starting to shape up," he realized.

"I'm not selling it," Josh said, as if staving off another argument.

"No, I think you should stay." Josh had been right all along—there was something here for him, just probably not what he'd originally expected. "This place suits you and the boys."

"Cloverville could suit you, too," his friend persisted.

Nick shook his head.

"I heard you looked at the Barber place."

"Small towns... Nothing goes unnoticed." He sighed. "I thought since there are no hotels, that it might be smart to have a place here. You know, for when the weather's bad."

Josh nodded. "Okay."

His friend's easy acceptance of his explanation didn't fool Nick. He avoided Josh's penetrating gaze and rubbed his hands over his face. "Not that I'll need it. I doubt I'll spend as much time in the office as you will."

"I heard you were already lining up appointments at the hardware store."

He laughed. "I didn't really have a choice. It was either that or Mr. Carpenter was going to take off his shirt so I could examine his shoulder. And Mrs. Hild…" He shook his head. She'd been too busy matchmaking to worry about her knees.

She'd thought he and Colleen would make the perfect couple. The old woman really shouldn't be so accepting of strangers. He'd probably hurt Colleen. Did she think he'd used her like that other guy had, the guy from her past?

The thought of any other man touching her, as Nick had touched her, knotted the muscles in his stomach. He had to stay away from Colleen, away from Cloverville. "Their appointments aside, I'm really not going to be at the office much. I'll mostly be at the hospital doing surgeries. Nothing has to change all that much."

"It already has," Josh said, his voice gentle, as if he didn't want to spook his friend. "*You've* changed."

Nick's guts twisted. Despite his efforts, Josh had scared him. "I haven't changed. We've just been here a week." But he'd made love to Colleen a couple of days ago.

"It's been long enough for you to fall in love," Josh mused.

"Don't make me hit you again," Nick threatened.

"You haven't taken a swing at me since I got drunk in college," Josh reminded him. Even though that wasn't the first time Nick had hit him. The first time had been when Josh had told him Bruce was in trouble, that he'd lost it and probably needed professional help. Josh acknowledged, "I had it coming, then."

"You do now, talking crazy." Nick shook his head. "I know

you don't have much of a sense of humor, but this isn't funny, even for you."

"I'm not trying to be funny, but you know that," Josh said. "I'm trying to have a serious discussion with my best friend because I'm afraid he's going to throw away his one shot at true happiness."

"One shot. You think that's all we get?"

Even though his eyes were serious, Josh laughed. "Not the rest of us. Only you. I've known you a long time, Nick, and you've never once let down your guard enough to fall in love."

"I didn't let down my guard." He bristled. "I can't."

Defensive, he knew he spewed nonsense, but he couldn't stem the flow of words. "She's just like Amy, like Molly, looking around the hospital for a husband. I'm not fool enough to fall for that mantrap."

Josh laughed again, unoffended. "You're not as stupid as I am, huh?"

Nick said nothing to contradict the conclusion his friend had drawn. He had thought Josh stupid to fall not once but twice for women who wanted him more because of his profession and money than his personality. Nick hoped like hell he hadn't made the same mistake himself. But it didn't matter. He didn't intend to act on his feelings for Colleen.

Josh's mouth twisted into a derisive grin. "You're an arrogant bastard."

"Hey!"

"And a gutless coward," Josh continued with the insults.

"You're really pushing me to hit you again," Nick threatened, his hand tightening around the handle of the paint roller.

"Come on, Nick. You're grasping at any excuse just because you're scared…."

He was. Of Colleen. Of his powerful, undeniable feelings

for her. But she was the woman he could least risk his heart on. If she turned out to be like the sister she idolized and she ran out on him, he'd be destroyed. Like Bruce had been destroyed. "I'm not husband material."

Josh laughed, with bitterness this time. "Apparently neither am I."

"Come on. You believe in this crap."

"Crap?"

"Love." He snorted. "Happiness."

Josh's laugh grew heartier. "Only you would call love and happiness crap."

"Anything that fleeting can only be crap."

"Nick, it doesn't have to be fleeting," Josh persisted. No wonder he kept trying—he was a hopeless romantic.

Nick was just hopeless. He shrugged. "I haven't seen any proof that it lasts."

"My parents—"

"Since that's the only example you've got, I'd call them a fluke. Look at all the people we work with, all the divorce horror stories we've heard."

"Our job. Our hours. It's hard on a relationship," Josh acknowledged. "That's why I wanted the private practice. We can set our own hours. As few—"

"Or as many as we want," Nick agreed.

"You're already pulling double shifts."

"I didn't have scholarships. I've got loans to pay off. And now we have another one."

"You won't regret opening the office here," Josh assured him.

But he was wrong. Nick already regretted coming to Cloverville and meeting Colleen, because he didn't know how he was going to forget her.

"For what it's worth, you're wrong about Colleen. But I

think you know that," Josh said. "If she has been volunteering in order to catch a husband, she would have been married long before now."

Nick's heart clenched painfully. He sucked in a breath but lowered his head so his friend wouldn't notice his reaction—to the nagging thought of Colleen with another man.

"It may have taken you a while," Josh taunted, "because you're slow. But other men have noticed her. You can't help but notice her, she's so beautiful."

"You?" He swallowed hard as jealousy rose like bile in his throat. "You asked her out?"

Josh nodded. "Just for coffee."

He curled his hand into a fist, even more tempted to hit his friend now than when Josh had been insulting him.

"She wasn't interested in me," Josh assured him. "She wasn't interested in anyone at the hospital."

Was she interested now? Despite her promise that she wouldn't fall for him, had she? Nick hoped not. He'd never intended to hurt her. "I have to get out of here."

"Yeah, you need a shower. That shade of green doesn't match your eyes," Josh teased.

His pulse quickening as if he were already running, he shook his head. "Not just here. I have to get out of Cloverville."

"I already told you I'm not leaving."

"I'm not asking you to leave. You're going to be fine here." But he wasn't. Like the colonel, he'd already lost his head—and maybe his heart. He had to leave before he lost his soul, too.

"You're not worried about me anymore?" Josh asked. "You've finally realized that I'm not Bruce?"

He hadn't fooled his friend—Josh knew why'd he'd been sticking around and what he'd been afraid of. "No, you're stronger." Than his brother. If only Nick could be certain that *he* was....

"You are, too," Josh insisted, friends so long that he'd probably read his mind.

Nick shook his head. "I don't think so. And I can't risk finding out."

COLLEEN LEANED AGAINST the doorjamb of Clayton's old bedroom, which, with tan paint and expensive bed linens, her mother had converted to an elegant guest room. Abby had been staying in it, but she apparently intended to change that. The petite blonde pulled clothes from the dresser and wadded the garments into balls in her suitcase. "What are you doing?"

Abby glanced up at the question. "I think it's obvious."

"But why are you leaving now?" Colleen asked. Abby couldn't take off when Colleen needed her friend most, when she'd gone and done something stupid again, like falling for a man who'd never love her back. "I thought you were actually considering moving here."

"Opening an office, yes. Moving here?" She sighed. "I considered it."

"I wish you'd open an office in Cloverville," Colleen said. "I could help you run it." Maybe working endless hours would help distract her...from Nick.

"Sure, Clayton would love that," Abby remarked with a derisive snort. "My stealing away his office manager."

"If he rented you the space next door..." Dr. Strover's old office. "I could manage both, with a little help. Mom even said she'd love working for you."

"Well, Clayton won't lease to me, so it doesn't matter."

"He's an idiot," Colleen said. Like Nick, he was afraid to

be around a woman for whom he might fall. Remembering her brother's moodiness, she figured it was probably too late for Clayton. He was just too stubborn to admit it. Like Nick? "You can lease a space somewhere else in Cloverville and I'll just quit him and come to work for you." As long as the office was nowhere near Nick's new building.

Abby laughed. "That'll make him love me." She snorted again. "Like that would ever happen."

Colleen's heart warmed. Abby loved Clayton, too—she was just scared that he'd never love her back. Colleen understood that fear well. "It won't if you take off."

"I don't want Clayton to…" She couldn't finish her protest.

"Abby, you're falling for Clayton." She clasped Abby's hand, so that she stopped packing. "That's wonderful."

"It's impossible. We hate each other."

"You know what they say about the fine line," Colleen teased. "Can you tell me that you really hate him?"

"No. But I wish I did."

"I understand." She wished she could hate Nick.

"I have to leave, Colleen."

She empathized. Part of her—the old impulsive part—wanted to run, too; to escape her feelings for Nick. But she'd accepted long ago that Cloverville was her home, and she had no intention of leaving her family or her friends. She had no intention of letting Abby leave, either. If she couldn't have her happily ever after, she'd make sure Abby finally got hers.

"You're leaving," remarked a male voice.

Nick turned from tossing stuff inside his duffel bag to glance over his shoulder at the man leaning against the door. His host wasn't particularly upset over losing his houseguest. In fact, he looked relieved.

As relieved as a man that tense could look, with his jaw clenched and his eyes ablaze with emotion. "You okay?" Nick asked him.

Clayton sighed. "Yeah, Colleen just told me something."

Nick closed his eyes, preparing himself for the beating he undoubtedly deserved.

"How could I have been so blind?" Clayton mused, his voice thick with self-recrimination.

Nick wondered that himself. Apparently everyone else had noticed his interest in Clayton's little sister. "I don't know what to say," he admitted. He had no excuse for taking advantage of Colleen.

Clayton laughed. "Of course you don't. You probably don't have a clue what I'm talking about."

Nick opened his eyes and studied the oldest McClintock sibling. "You're talking about Colleen."

"And Abby," Clayton added with a ragged sigh.

Nick nodded as realization dawned. "She told you about the colonel."

"You knew?"

He shrugged. "Small towns."

"Everyone knew but me?"

"No. Colleen told me," he admitted. "I think she'd gotten tired of carrying around her secret—and the guilt."

"She shouldn't have felt guilty."

"No, she shouldn't have. Is she okay?" Nick had to know. He'd always been aware how much Colleen's family meant to her. It couldn't have been easy for her to tell her older brother about her youthful indiscretion.

Clayton nodded. "She's not really happy with me right now, though."

"Maybe you need to start giving her more responsibility

around here," he suggested. "You must realize how smart she is. And strong." Stronger than he was.

"I do now. I wish she would have told me then," her brother said, his voice tinged with regret, "but I probably wouldn't have believed her. Or even listened to the poor girl in the first place."

"You feel guilty." Nick recognized the emotion he, too, had lived with for so long—until Colleen had made him see he couldn't have changed anything about the past. Bruce wouldn't have listened to him; he'd always seen Nick as a kid.

"I already apologized to Colleen," Clayton said, "but I owe someone else a huge apology."

Amusement lifted Nick's lips. "Abby."

"I was the one carrying the torch when the angry mob ran her out of town." Clayton obviously exaggerated.

Nick laughed at the picture the other man had painted. "I don't think it was quite like that. From what I've heard, she'd always intended to leave anyway."

Clayton sighed. "Yeah, she'd made it clear she hated living here." He gestured toward Nick's bag. "So you're leaving?"

He nodded. "Yeah."

Clayton heaved a sigh of relief.

Nick laughed. "Obviously, I've taken advantage of your hospitality."

"It's not that," Clayton explained. "I asked Abby to come over. I need to offer her an apology that's eight years too late."

Nick suspected the other man would give Abby Hamilton more than an apology. The poor bastard was obviously in love. Grabbing up his haphazardly packed duffel bag, Nick joined Clayton near the door and extended his hand. "I wish you luck, man."

Clayton shook his hand. "Thanks. We're talking about Abby here, so I know damned well that I'm going to need it."

Nick stepped into the hall and headed toward the door, but Clayton's question stopped him.

"What about you, Nick?"

Nick turned back and asked, "What about me?"

"Did you find what you need in Cloverville?" Clayton shook his head, as if answering his own question. "Of course you didn't. You wouldn't be leaving if you had."

Actually, he was leaving because he *had*. He didn't want to need anyone the way he needed Colleen—the way his brother had needed his wife. She'd betrayed him. She'd stopped loving him.

Colleen had said she didn't love Nick yet, but he knew she could. She could stop loving him, too. And Nick knew, like his brother, he wouldn't survive a broken heart.

Chapter Thirteen

"I thought I might find you here."

Colleen brushed away the tears that were streaming from her eyes before she turned away from the colonel to face Nick. "You know what they say about always returning to the scene of the crime."

He shook his head. "I thought you'd agreed to give yourself a break."

She forced a smile. "I did. I have. But I just told Clayton the truth." And she'd been overwhelmed by all the emotions, guilt, regret and, finally, relief. It was over. Everyone knew now.

"I just talked to him," Nick said, grasping the handle of the duffel bag he carried. "He was getting ready to apologize to Abby for having misjudged her."

"Good." Satisfaction joined the relief. "It's a long-overdue apology."

"He seemed really anxious to talk to her."

Her lips curved into a smile. She'd put pressure on Clayton to convince Abby to stay in Cloverville. "Maybe I'm more like my mom than I thought."

His forehead furrowed as he obviously tried to follow her change of subject. But he'd probably rather talk about anything other than the reason he carried the duffel bag stuffed with his belongings, so he asked, "How are you like your mother?"

"I'm playing matchmaker," she explained.

"You don't seem the type to meddle."

"I'm not," she agreed then laughed. "I'm usually too self-involved to worry about other people's lives."

"Right," he said, his voice tinged with irony. "That's why you volunteer in the pediatric cancer ward."

"I do that because I'm trying to land a rich doctor," she told him with an exaggerated wink.

"Colleen!"

"That's what you want to believe," she said.

"Yes," he admitted. "I want to, but you're messing that up. You're messing *me* up, Colleen."

"Is that why you're leaving?" Even if she hadn't noticed his bag, she would have known he'd come to say goodbye. The word was there in his serious green eyes, on his unsmiling lips.

"Yes."

She flinched over the ache in her heart. "Thanks for not lying to me."

"I never lied to you," he promised.

She lifted a brow, skeptical. "Not even when you were trying to charm Molly's whereabouts out of me?"

"Every word I said was true," he insisted. Nick had tried to convince himself he was only seeing her to con her sister's whereabouts out of her. But he'd been looking for any reason to see more of her, to spend more time with her. What a fool he'd been. Or maybe he was the bigger fool now that he'd decided to leave.

She nodded. "Sure, every word you said…"

"You are so beautiful."

If that were all she was, Nick would have no problem

walking away and leaving her behind. But she was so much more. Caring, smart, generous… Sensitive.

Eyes narrowed, she studied him. "I believe you mean that."

She believed he meant it, but not that she actually was beautiful. He dropped the heavy bag to reach for her, cupping her face in his palms. He ran his thumbs along the line of her cheekbones, her jaw, then across her full, sexy lips. "Believe that you are."

"I will." Her breath whispered across his skin.

He had to kiss her. One last time. He touched his mouth to hers, melting into the softness and heat. She tasted so sweet, like peaches and cream.

Her fingers grasped his shirt, pulling him closer as she stretched her arms over his shoulders. "Nick…"

She knew it. He heard it in her voice. The resignation. The acceptance. This would be their last time together.

"Colleen, I want you." He slid his hand to her shoulders, the bones delicate beneath the cotton blouse she wore with shorts that left her long, sexy legs bare.

She smiled as she said, "So, take me."

He laughed at her audacity. She never failed to surprise him. How could anyone have ignored her—how had he ignored her? "In the middle of a public park?"

"We almost made love here once before," she reminded him.

He couldn't believe how quickly he'd fallen for her, how badly he'd wanted her that day. And today, he wanted her even more. That was why he had to leave—before he got in any deeper. Before he found himself unable to live without her.

She slid her hands from his shoulders to the nape of his neck, kneading the tense muscles before pulling him down for another kiss. "If not here, where?" she murmured the question against his lips.

He grasped her hips, pulling her tight against his aching body. "I was thinking about a hotel."

She kissed him again, her lips clinging, her tongue slipping inside to tease. Breathing hard, she reminded him, "There are no hotels in Cloverville."

"What about Grand Rapids?"

What about taking her home with him? No, he couldn't. He didn't want her in that part of his life. And if he brought her to his condo he'd see her in every room, forever feel her in his bed. In his arms.

"There are hotels there," she agreed, teasingly misunderstanding his question, "but we'll both come to our senses during the drive. We'll realize that we should have just shaken hands and said goodbye."

He shifted his hips against her, so that she'd feel the erection straining against the fly of his jeans. So she'd know he was about to lose his head again for wanting her.

"I don't want to shake hands with you." Nothing so impersonal—like strangers meeting at a wedding might do. They hadn't been strangers since the moment they'd met. "I need to touch you." To bury himself inside her, to lose himself in her heat and passion… Just one more time.

"We'll go back in the woods—so you won't have to worry about the colonel or anyone else interrupting us."

He wouldn't miss this odd little town. Sure he'd have to come back, take some appointments at the office in order to hold up his end of the partnership with Josh. But he'd stay on the side of town where he'd insisted they build, where there were only new developments. He would avoid the park and all the busybodies who gossiped on Main Street. He wouldn't want to hear about Colleen if he wasn't going to let himself see her again.

Still he had to know. "Why hasn't the town ever had him

properly fixed?" He was a welder's son, and he could see that someone had only haphazardly soldered together the colonel's broken joints.

Colleen lifted her delicate shoulders in a shrug. "Mr. Carpenter was mayor for quite a while, and he didn't like spending money on anything. Do you really want to talk about the colonel?"

He shook his head. "No, I don't want to talk at all."

Her hand traveled down his arm until she linked their fingers. Then she tugged him toward the woods.

"You're not running," he mused as he followed her down an overgrown trail to a small clearing. But this was where she used to come, he'd bet, when she'd run away from home. Even if they'd looked, nobody would have been able to find her— not this deep in the woods. No one would interrupt them.

Her voice hushed, she murmured, "No, I'm not the one running away."

He was. They both knew that, too. "Colleen, I wish…"

She rose up on tiptoe and pressed her mouth to his. She didn't want to hear wishes she knew he had no intention of fulfilling. But that was okay. She'd resigned herself to taking what he could give her, and if it was only this—mind-blowing pleasure—she'd take that and be grateful.

His hands moved down her back, over the curve of her butt to the backs of her thighs, and now his fingers played with the hem of her shorts. He teased her with fleeting touches.

She wanted his hands—everywhere. She leaned back, grasping his T-shirt in her hands. Then she dragged the shirt over his head, exposing his muscular chest to her hungry gaze. She slid her mouth over him, teasing his small nipples until they hardened. When she flicked her tongue over them, his breath hissed out, stirring her hair.

He slid his hands into her shorts, under her panties and over the curve of her bare backside. "You have on too many clothes," he complained.

He quickly remedied that situation, unsnapping and pulling down her denim shorts and then slipping off her panties. Then he reached for the buttons on her blouse. Colleen let him undress her, let him take his time, brushing her skin with his knuckles, tasting each exposed inch with his mouth.

Her knees weakened and trembled, so she locked her arms around his waist and held on. She wanted to hold on to him forever. But he didn't want that. And, truthfully, neither did she. It was better that this was their last time and that they were saying goodbye. Then she wouldn't risk falling any harder. Better to lose him now than in the way her mother had lost her father, after years of loving each other.

His hair, so silky soft, brushed against her breasts as he lowered his head. His lips closed over a nipple and he tugged gently. Pleasure flowed throughout Colleen, and she moaned. But his mouth wasn't enough. She had to have all of him.

She reached for his jeans, unzipping them and pushing them down so she could touch him, could stroke her fingers over the hard length of him.

He groaned against her breast. "You're driving me crazy…"

She tangled her fingers in his silky hair and tugged his head up, then sealed her mouth to his, plunging her tongue through his lips, tasting him. He was dark, rich and somewhat bitter, like espresso. And like espresso, he had her pulse racing, her heart skipping beats.

His fingers slid inside her, teasing her as she'd just teased him. Instead of biting her lip to hold in a moan, she bit his lips, then stroked her tongue over the nip she'd inflicted.

"You're bad," he said without complaint, closing his eyes

and groaning as she stroked her hand up and down the length of his erection.

She shook her head. "You ain't seen nothing yet." Then she replaced her fingers with her lips, taking him deep inside her mouth as she knelt in front of him.

"Colleen!" he shouted her name, and as he did, birds rustled the tree limbs overhead before escaping with a flap of their wings to open sky.

Wasn't he doing the same thing? Escaping?

Colleen wanted to make it hard for him to forget her. But his fingers grasped her arms, pulling her to her feet. Then his mouth was everywhere. At her throat. Her breasts. He dropped to his knees in the middle of the field, and he put his mouth against her.

Sensations slammed through her. Pleasure so intense she shuddered as it coursed through her body. She tangled her fingers in his hair again, first clutching him against her and then pulling him away.

He caught her, dragging her down with him onto the grass and weeds. Then he was inside her, buried so deep inside that she knew, no matter if she never saw him again, he would always be a part of her. She clutched him, her nails digging into his shoulders and her heels pressed against the back of his thighs as she rose to match his frantic thrusts.

They climaxed together, moaning each other's names. Colleen's throat burned with the intensity of her cry—of her pleasure. Of the loss she already felt, even though he was still inside her.

His face against her throat, he murmured, "Are you okay?"

She could only nod.

"I didn't hurt you?"

"No…" If he'd made her feel any better, she'd be dead.

"No twigs digging into your back?"

She shook her head and then cleared her throat. "I think we could be lying in poison ivy, though."

His chest vibrated against her breasts as he laughed. "We're going to need shots."

"Just what you want to hear after making love."

"Colleen…"

"It's okay," she assured him. "I've never been allergic to poison ivy." And growing up in Cloverville, she'd been around enough of it. When she'd run away, she'd often come to this clearing and lain in the grass.

Nick eased back and leaned his forehead against hers. His pale green eyes held more remorse than poison ivy required. "I'm sorry."

"Why?" She cupped his face in her hands and kissed his lips. "I don't regret what we did—either the other day or now."

"Seriously, Colleen, you have no regrets?"

She shook her head.

"Are you sure?" he persisted.

Her breath hitched, as she admitted, "I had a crush on you."

"Had?" His lips lifted in a grin even as a muscle twitched in his jaw. "Did I crush your crush?"

She shook her head. "No. I think I've outgrown crushes. My first crush was on Eric South." She emitted a wistful sigh.

"Eric South?"

If she didn't know better, she'd almost think his voice had roughened with jealousy when he'd repeated the name. "He's a really good friend, more Molly's than mine. If he'd agreed, I'm sure Molly would have asked him to be her maid of honor or had him as her best man."

"I don't remember meeting him at the wedding. But since they were so close, he must have been there."

She shook her head. "He was supposed to be one of the groomsmen, but he backed out."

"So if your sister ran to someone, she'd run to him?"

She shrugged. "I thought that you didn't care anymore where my sister is."

"I don't," he insisted. "For some reason I'm more interested in your old crushes."

"Like I said, I outgrew the one on Eric. Then there was…" Even now, all these years later, her face heated when she said his name. "Jimmy Hendrix."

"The musician? Aren't you a little young…"

She shook her head. "The quarterback. And bad boy." Older brother to the bad boys Rory had hung around with, until either she or Abby had gotten through to him. "Irresistible combination." But she wished she had resisted him.

"He's the one who hurt your pride?"

She nodded. "So I got over my crush on him. And now I've outgrown my crush on you."

"Colleen…"

"Don't worry. I don't love you," she assured him. She'd disclosed one secret only to keep another. But she'd tell no one of her love for Dr. Nick Jameson. There was no point in loving him. Except pain.

Pain flashed through Nick, pressing on his heart. He wanted her love? He didn't deserve it, and he'd done nothing to earn it. "I'm sorry," he said again. Sorry that she didn't love him, even though it was better that she didn't. For her. He didn't want her running into anything ever again.

"I told you. It's okay," she assured him. "You can't force yourself to feel something you don't."

Or force himself *not* to feel something he did. But he had to try to get over her. He couldn't do it here in Cloverville where he'd probably see her every day, no matter if he stayed in her brother's guest room or Josh's freshly painted one.

"I have to leave."

She slid her hands over his face, her palms soft against his skin. "It's okay. I'm used to people leaving me."

"I wish things could be different. I wish I could be different for you. I wish I could be the man you deserve." Someone she'd fall in love with and love forever. But he wasn't half the man his brother had been. Half the man Josh was. If women couldn't love those two men forever, he didn't have a chance.

Chapter Fourteen

The words on the page blurred as Colleen hunched over the library table and tried to read the book she'd picked up. But there were no receptive listeners here. She read silently, evaluating the story as one she might bring to the hospital. If she dared to go back to the hospital…

She knew why Nick had left Cloverville—to get away from her. If she followed him back to Grand Rapids, he would think she was chasing him, just as he feared. He would think she wanted more from him than he could give.

And he'd be right.

Everyone, even his best friend, had warned her about Nick Jameson's aversion to love and commitment, but still she'd fallen in love. She understood his reasons for remaining uninvolved. After seeing a woman crush the older brother he'd idolized and watching two other women betray his best friend, he didn't trust any woman to keep her promises. And he probably had more reason to mistrust her than most women. She'd kept secrets; she'd acted impulsively. But falling for Nick Jameson had been the most impulsive thing she'd ever done.

"Stupid, stupid," she murmured, pressing the heel of her palm against her forehead.

"Hey, don't talk about my sister that way," whispered a feminine voice from behind Colleen's shoulder.

Colleen's heart leaped with relief as she whipped her head around. "Molly!"

"Shh…" The command came from her sister's lips, not the librarian who slumped behind the front desk, snoring. Colleen and Molly were the only ones—awake—in the library this late in the evening.

Colleen pushed her chair back from the table and launched herself at her older sister, pulling the smaller woman into her arms. "Thank God, you're home!"

"Yes, I'm home." Molly pulled back and glanced around the library as if it were the sanctuary she'd been seeking.

But Colleen doubted her sister had spent the entire week and a half she'd been gone inside these walls. "So did you leave town? We all thought you were with Eric."

"I don't want to talk about Eric," Molly said, her eyes clouding with sadness.

Obviously Colleen wasn't the only McClintock with a seriously hurting heart. She didn't want to pry, but Eric had been a friend too long for her not to ask. "Is he okay?"

Molly sighed. "Yes. Poor Colleen, you always had a crush on him."

"Poor Eric," she sympathized. "He always had a crush on you."

Her big eyes damp with misery, she said, "Not anymore."

"What's going on, Molly?"

With dark circles rimming her brown eyes and her usually honey-toned skin pale, Molly looked more than three years older than Colleen. Unlike Colleen, who wore her usual work uniform of a blouse and skirt, Molly had on a knit and lace camisole with jean shorts, probably something she'd packed for her honeymoon. She'd had the suitcase in her car when she'd run away from the church, from her wedding.

"Are you okay?" Colleen asked, still amazed that Molly— sensible, responsible Molly—had taken off the way she had: out a window minutes before she was supposed to have walked down the aisle and said, *I do*.

Her sister nodded, dark curls bouncing around her bare shoulders. "Yes. I'm fine. I'm really sorry…"

"No, you don't need to apologize. You've been under so much pressure for years, with college and medical school. Sometimes you just need to take off." No one understood that better than Colleen. "So your time alone—it worked?" she asked. "You figured out what you want?"

Molly nodded again. "I figured it out, but that doesn't mean I'll get it."

"So what do you want?" Eric?

Her eyes shimmering, Molly shook her head. "Can we talk about it later?" she asked as she settled onto the edge of the table near where Colleen had piled books. She picked up one of them and glanced at the title. "You're picking out books to read the kids at the hospital?"

Colleen nodded. She was picking them out, but she didn't know if she'd actually get to read them.

"Good choices," Molly approved. She'd always loved books and had passed that love on to her younger sister by reading to her and then teaching her to read when they were kids. Her voice hesitant, Molly asked, "So you've seen Josh?"

"Not at the hospital," Colleen said. She wasn't the only one who hadn't been there. "Josh is still on…"

Molly's face flushed with color. "Our honeymoon?"

Colleen shook her head. She hadn't known their honeymoon destination. "He didn't go anywhere. He stayed in Cloverville, him and Buzz and TJ."

"Where has he stayed?" Molly asked, her voice shaky with nerves. "Our house?"

She'd obviously not been home yet.

"With the Kellys," Colleen said, "but just until he gets the Manning house livable for him and the boys."

"He bought the Manning house?" Obviously she and her groom hadn't talked all that much before their wedding and not at all after their wedding-that-wasn't. Maybe he'd intended the house as a surprise though, as a wedding present.

"Josh is moving here," Colleen reminded her sister, letting her know that Molly running out on him hadn't changed his plans. "He and Nick are opening their office. It'll be done soon." And then Nick would be back in Cloverville, on the other side of town. She doubted he'd stop by the insurance office or the park again. He wouldn't want to run the risk of seeing her.

"I've made such a mess of things," Molly said, shaking her head as she grimaced in self-disgust.

Colleen laughed.

"Hey, it's not funny!"

Colleen held up her palms in a placating gesture. "I'm sorry. It's just that I'm used to you being perfect and me being the screwup."

"*I've* never been the perfect one," Molly insisted. "There's only been one perfect McClintock."

"Clayton?"

Molly shook her head. "No, he can be a real pain in the ass. Especially for Abby."

That had changed, but Abby should be the one to share the news of her engagement with her friend. Colleen suppressed the grin at the thought of Abby becoming her sister-in-law. For years, she'd already felt like her sister.

"And the perfect McClintock is certainly not Rory," Molly continued, "the little hellion."

Colleen defended her younger brother. "He's actually started to straighten up." Since their talk that night on the back patio.

"I was talking about you, Colleen. You've always been the perfect one."

She'd forgotten that one person still didn't know her secret. "I'm a long way from perfect, Mol. There's something you don't know—"

"I know about you and the colonel," Molly interrupted.

"Abby told you?"

She shook her head. "No, Abby would take a friend's secret to her grave. *You* told us. You were so miserable and guilty when she took off." Molly squeezed her shoulder. "She was going to leave anyway, she'd always planned to take off, but we couldn't convince you of that."

"So you *all* knew my secret?" she asked.

"That secret," she said dismissively as if it hadn't mattered.

And Colleen finally realized that it really hadn't. Abby was fine. Everyone was fine but her.

"Tell me your new secret," Molly urged. As her older sister, she must have instinctively picked up that Colleen had another one.

"I don't know what you're talking about," Colleen said, stalling.

"Tell me what has you sitting alone in the library, trying not to cry," her sister persisted.

Colleen forced a smile. "I'm not crying."

Molly arched an eyebrow, obviously not buying Colleen's claim.

"Really."

"What's his name?" Molly asked.

After keeping one for so long, apparently for no good reason, Colleen was sick of secrets, so she took a deep breath and spilled. "Nick."

Molly's eyes widened with sympathy. "Oh, no, it's worse than I thought."

"Certainly hopeless," Colleen agreed.

"Then, you know—" her sister pitched her voice low "—how he feels about marriage?"

Colleen glanced toward the librarian, who slept on, and after that she didn't bother whispering her fatalistic "Yes."

"But you still fell for him," Molly concluded.

"Like I told you, I'm a long way from perfect."

"No, you're human, Colleen. And we can't help who we fall in love with." Molly slid off the table to settle wearily into one of the wing chairs, which was upholstered in a book-patterned fabric. "I realize that now."

"You know, I seriously think he could love me, too." Colleen had begun to see herself as he had. She was beautiful. She was smart. Loving. "He just has to let himself."

Molly blinked hard, as if fighting tears of her own, when she commiserated, "Men can be so damned stubborn."

Colleen nodded in agreement. "I know."

Molly squeezed her hand in sympathy. "I'm so sorry, honey, that you're hurting."

"It's okay." And she realized that it was. "I'm strong enough to handle a broken heart." Too bad it had taken a broken heart for her to realize exactly how strong she was.

"DR. JAMESON, YOU CAME back from your vacation early," remarked one of the nurses as he approached the nursing station outside the surgery waiting rooms.

He didn't know her name. He'd always made it a point to never learn them. Now he glanced at the tag on her scrubs. "Melanie. I wanted to be back at work."

"I thought you were going into private practice. Or has that changed now that…"

"No. Dr. Towers and I are still opening our own office. But I'll continue to be on staff here."

"For surgeries, of course."

"And on call." He couldn't cut back on his hours as Josh planned to do. He had no little boys to fill his time. An image of Colleen's face, animated, as she read to Buzz and TJ flashed through his mind—one of the many images of her he carried with him, even though he'd left her behind. Someday, she'd be a wonderful mother.

"I heard about what happened," Melanie said quietly, and glanced around the bustling corridor, "with Dr. Towers's wedding, being jilted right at the altar like that. Is he all right?"

Finally fully believing it himself, Nick assured her, "He'll be fine."

He wasn't so sure about himself, though. Getting back to work had done nothing to help him get over his feelings for Colleen. Because even though she wasn't at the hospital, he could imagine her there. He could almost feel her presence, her sweet, generous energy.

"I don't really know Molly McClintock," the nurse continued. "She hasn't been volunteering here as long as her younger sister, and being in med school she's not around that often."

"Colleen." His heart clenched. It hurt just to say her name.

"Yes, Colleen." Melanie's voice warmed with affection. "I hope she comes back soon. The kids are asking for her. They really miss her."

The kids weren't the only ones.

She laughed. "Not just the kids are missing her."

Had he gotten that easy to read?

"Dr. Adams keeps asking when she's coming back."

"Dr. Adams is married." And at least twice her age. He fisted his hands, tempted to go find Dr. Adams.

Melanie nodded seriously in agreement, even as her eyes gleamed with excitement at this chance for gossip. "That hasn't stopped him from asking her out."

Nick regretted that he hadn't listened to gossip before. "Is he the only one?" he asked.

"Who's asked out Colleen?" She laughed, then lowered her voice to a conspiratorial whisper. She rivaled Mr. Carpenter and Mrs. Hild. "Not hardly. I think every male in the hospital has asked her out." Her face colored. "Well, except for you."

"Yes, except for me." He'd been a fool to never notice her before.

"Colleen reminds me of you," Melanie remarked.

He was aware they had a lot in common, but he wondered about the nurse's observation. "How's that?"

"She never accepted any of those invitations, so she must have decided, like you, not to date anyone from the hospital."

He'd considered that one of his smarter decisions until now. By ignoring Colleen until the wedding, he'd wasted so much time. And he'd wasted even more since he'd left Cloverville. Distance wasn't going to make a difference; it wasn't going to weaken or erase his feelings for her.

He'd long ago come to the same conclusion as Melanie, that he and Colleen had a lot in common. For far too long they had both lived with pain over the losses in their past. They had allowed fear to affect their future. If they figured out how to let it go—the pain *and* the fear—could they have a future together?

"I'm sorry, Doctor," the nurse said, "I've rambled on and on, and I know how you hate gossip. I must have bored you to death talking about Colleen McClintock."

Nothing about Colleen would ever bore him. "It's fine. Really," he assured her.

"You had a question for me."

He could barely remember what it was. "Yeah, I'd like to talk to the paramedics who brought in Westin."

"Was there a problem?" she asked, her expression guarded as if protecting one of them. "I thought the surgery went well, that he'll have a full recovery."

"There's no problem at all," he explained. "Whoever worked on him at the scene of the accident saved his leg, at least, but probably his life, too. Damned fine work." He'd seen work like that before and figured the paramedic had more medical training than just his Emergency Medical Tech courses. He'd just been too self-absorbed—as Colleen had accused herself of being—to seek out and compliment the paramedic.

"That was Eric South."

He'd heard the name before—on Colleen's lips. Jealousy dimmed some of his admiration for the guy, the one on whom Colleen had had her first crush. His every thought always came back to her. Nick's pulse quickened.

"He might still be in the staff lounge. His shift was over, but he waited for word on how Westin's surgery went. I let him know you were your usual brilliant self," she gushed.

He ignored her compliment and headed toward the lounge. He paused in the doorway, letting a couple of nurses pass him on their way out. They hesitated, as if trying to catch his attention, but he ignored them, too.

Only one person occupied the lounge now. A guy with dark

blond hair stood in front of the coffeepot, his back to Nick. "Eric?"

The guy turned only fractionally, meeting Nick's gaze over his shoulder. His eyes, a steely gray, flickered with recognition. "Yeah. Hey, Doctor, do you need something?"

"I thought you were off the clock."

Broad shoulders shrugged. "I've got no place else to be."

"I hear you," Nick commiserated. He could find no place to escape thoughts of Colleen.

South sighed. "But I've got no one but myself to blame."

"I hear you," Nick repeated. He'd had a choice. He could have stayed in Cloverville—with Colleen. But he'd chosen to run.

"You know my name, Eric South," the other man said, as he turned fully and extended the hand not holding a coffee mug to Nick.

Nick hesitated a moment before taking the hand and offering his name. Not because of any residual jealousy. The long, jagged scar on Eric's left cheek had drawn all his attention. And concern. "Nick Jameson."

Eric released his hand, then touched his scar—not self-consciously but as if used to people staring at it. "You should see the other guy."

Nick visually examined the scar and evaluated it. "A fist didn't do that damage. I'd say jagged metal, maybe glass fragments. Car accident?" Had he been in the car when Colleen struck the colonel?

"It was no accident," Eric said, his voice hoarse. "Afghanistan."

"How long have you been back?" Although the scar didn't look fresh, South might have had a good reason for missing Josh's wedding—a better reason than the bride could have had. But this man needed to see Josh, who'd undoubtedly have some ideas about how to repair the man's scar.

"I've been back a couple of years."

Nick nodded. "You were a medic over there." Now he understood the paramedic's skill.

"Yes, with the Marine Corps."

"You did a good job with Westin."

Eric nodded. "Heard you did, too."

Nick shrugged. He didn't want to discuss the surgery, which would have shocked the hell out of Josh who often got sick of shoptalk.

"Couldn't have been easy," the paramedic continued.

Nick's arrogance had his chin whipping up. Even if a surgery were hard, he'd rarely admit it was. "No…"

"Because of your poison ivy," Eric explained, gesturing toward the rash that could be seen on Nick's arms. "I break out every time I set foot near Cloverville Park."

Nick glanced down at his rash, remembering how he'd gotten it. He didn't regret anything but leaving. "I gave myself a cortisone injection and made sure I wasn't contagious before I came back to work."

South nodded. "Still damned uncomfortable. So where'd you get it?"

"Cloverville Park. But you knew that," Nick surmised.

The corners of Eric's mouth lifted, the right side higher than the left, into a grin. "You're the other one of the *GQ* docs."

Nick's jaw tightened. He really hated that nickname.

South nodded. "You're the best man. Gossip around town is that you were spending time with Colleen McClintock."

Not nearly enough time. "I should have known someone would hear about us."

"There are no secrets in Cloverville."

Nick grinned. "No, there aren't. You were supposed to be in the wedding party, too."

Eric nodded. "Yup, but there was no wedding."

"No, there wasn't." And Nick suspected Eric South was a big part of the reason. "So you're where Molly McClintock was staying."

Eric nodded. "She's gone home now."

Maybe it was time Nick went home, too. To Cloverville. And Colleen.

Chapter Fifteen

Unable to sleep, just as she'd been every night since Nick had come to Cloverville, Colleen had risen at dawn and left for the park. Usually at this hour of the morning she had it to herself—just her and the colonel until Mr. Meisner brought Lolly for her morning walk.

But today she stepped through the gates to a cacophony of metal clanging against metal and the hiss of a torch. Occasionally—when the colonel's head fell off—teenagers took it and positioned it in other areas of town. On top of mailboxes and the order-taking speaker of the drive-through window, for example. But no one had ever entirely dismantled the statue before. Although no one but her apparently cared, she'd already hurt their proud town founder; no one else should be allowed to do him more harm. She ran over to the colonel and yelled at the man who was welding. "Hey! What are you doing?"

The man shut off his torch, turned to her and lifted his welder's mask. Pale green eyes gleamed in a dirty face. "Hello, there."

If not for the wrinkles rimming his eyes and circling his jaw, the man could have been Nick. And he wasn't dismantling the colonel; he'd actually been putting him back together. Properly.

"Hello?" she said, befuddled by his presence in Cloverville, in this park.

His pale eyes twinkled. "You're Colleen McClintock."

"You know who I am?" she asked, surprised. "Were you at the wedding?" She remembered Nick saying that Josh had named one of twins, TJ—Thomas Joshua—after Nick's dad, so he'd undoubtedly been invited to the wedding.

He grimaced. "No, I was driving in for it, but I got caught in a traffic jam. Then Nick gave me a call on the cell phone the boy insisted that I have, and he told me to forget about it, that..."

"My sister had gone out the window?" she guessed.

He smiled. "So I turned around and missed out on the fun. I would have liked to have a dance with a pretty girl like you."

"How do you know who I am?" she wondered.

"My son described you well."

"He didn't have to describe you," she said. "He looks so much like you."

He lifted his chin, as if offended. "Of course, I'm better looking."

"Of course," she agreed, and couldn't help but smile. "You're Thomas Jameson."

The older man grinned. "Only my mother ever called me Thomas, and usually when I was in trouble." He winked before adding, "I was in trouble a lot. It's Tommy to you, honey."

Colleen's smile widened. She saw now where Nick had inherited his charm. "Tommy, it's nice to meet you."

The old man whistled. "Nicky didn't do you justice. You're even more beautiful than he said."

Now she laughed. "He didn't warn me about what a flirt you are."

But then he hadn't ever expected her to meet his father. He'd left Cloverville because he wanted nothing more to do with her. She blinked back the threat of tears, but she couldn't suppress the sting of pain over his rejection.

"I don't understand what you're doing here," she admitted.

He lifted the blackened torch toward the colonel, whose head had been reattached. Even his hat and ear had been fixed so they were no longer dented and mangled. "Fixing this proud old soldier."

Colleen sighed. For years the city council had refused to spend the money to properly fix the colonel. Mr. Carpenter hadn't been the only spendthrift; Clayton, as a town council member, hadn't wanted to repair the colonel, either. She realized now that he'd wanted a reminder of what he'd considered Abby's carelessness. He'd wanted a reason to not fall in love with her. Since he'd finally admitted his love and put their mother's old engagement ring on Abby's finger, he must have decided it was past time to repair the town founder. "It's long overdue."

"That's what my son thought," Tommy Jameson said.

"So the town council didn't hire you?"

He shook his head, rattling the welder's mask. "No. Nicky did. Tried paying me, too, that crazy kid."

Crazy kid? The serious, no-nonsense Dr. Jameson? No one at the hospital would have believed his father's description of him.

"Nick asked you to come here from Grand Rapids?" she asked.

"Detroit, honey. I still live in Detroit, where I raised Nicky and his older brother, Bruce. He wants me to move, says the neighborhood's getting bad." He shrugged. "Maybe it is. Maybe I'll consider moving now. This sure is a pretty town. But I really like being close to Evelyn."

"Evelyn?" she repeated, reeling from all the information he'd divulged. Nick had grown up in Detroit?

"Evelyn, the boys' mom."

Of course. Nick had never told her anything about his mother. Or really about the rest of his family. His father's name had only been mentioned in passing, when he'd told her the twins' name: And what he'd told her about Bruce had probably been intended more as a warning than a confidence.

"She won't consider moving?" Colleen asked.

Tommy's eyes dimmed with sadness. "She's dead, honey. Died shortly after Nicky was born."

As if it hadn't been bad enough that Nick had lost his older brother, he'd already lost his mother before that. "I'm sorry."

"If it wasn't for his brother, Bruce, and my mother, God rest her soul—" the old man lifted his eyes heavenward "—I don't know how I would have managed. Nicky always was a handful."

"I didn't know." Because Nick hadn't told her. No wonder he didn't trust women—he'd never known any who'd stuck around. Of course his mother hadn't left by choice, but she wondered if Nick understood that.

"Oh, I think you know that the boy's a lot of work," Tommy said, obviously misunderstanding her remark. "He can try the patience of a saint."

She glanced up at the mended statue of Colonel Clover. "I'm no saint."

"Good," he replied with satisfaction. "You'd only bore my son if you were."

Her face heated with embarrassment. "Oh, no. We're not together. You have the wrong idea about us."

"If I have the wrong idea, honey—" his pale eyes gleamed with affection "—it's because Nicky gave it to me."

"I don't know why he'd do that…" Not when he'd made it clear he wanted nothing to do with her.

The older man shrugged. "Then you should ask him to

explain himself, because for the first time in a long time, I think the boy has finally got things figured out."

Things? What about Colleen and his feelings for her? Had he figured those out? And if he had, why tell his father before he told her?

Of course she'd assured him that she hadn't fallen in love with him. She'd lied to him; she'd kept her secret. Maybe it was time that Colleen stopped avoiding Nick and gave him a piece of her mind. It was only fitting since he already had her heart.

THE DOOR TO NICK'S APARTMENT crashed open, banging against the wall and drawing his attention from the box he was packing. The cat, its calico hair raised up like when the boys visited, streaked across the carpet toward the hall and probably the bottom of the linen closet, where it liked to hide.

"Hey, if you're a thief, you're not very subtle," he remarked to whoever had broken into his place. "Did I leave the door unlocked?"

Because he hadn't, the intruder had to be someone he knew. Only two people had keys to his condo—Josh and his dad. The soft footsteps didn't sound as though they belonged to either one of them. His pulse quickened, not with fear but anticipation. He couldn't see his intruder until she came around the pile of already packed boxes filling his apartment. Then his breath left his lungs. "Colleen."

"Josh loaned me his key."

His best friend might have called Nick, warned him that she was coming. So that he could have been prepared to see her again. Only a few days had passed since he'd left Cloverville but he'd missed her so much. How could he have forgotten the exact shade of her hair, of her eyes…the pale silk of her skin. She was so damned beautiful.

"Well, to be honest…" she said.

And he believed she was always honest.

"I didn't give him much choice."

"Who?" Him. She'd left him with no choice but to fall in love with her. At first sight.

"I left Josh no choice about giving me your key and directions to the condo." She glanced around as if just noticing the boxes. "You're moving?"

He nodded.

Her enormous eyes darkened with pain. "What? Grand Rapids isn't far enough for you to get away from me?" She blew out an agitated breath. "Now I'm even angrier with you."

"You're angry with me? I wouldn't have guessed from the way you broke down the door," he teased, loving her feistiness.

She ignored him, her attention focused on the packed boxes. "Where are you going?"

"I'm moving *to* Cloverville," he explained. "I bought the Barber house."

"But you *hate* Cloverville. You never wanted to open the office there."

"I was wrong." And not just about Cloverville. "But why are you angry with me?"

She sucked in a breath, as startled as if he'd slapped her. "You admitted you were wrong?"

He laughed. "Yeah, Josh has been rubbing it in, too." How the mighty have fallen and all that. He probably deserved it; he'd been an arrogant, above-it-all jerk for too long. Until he'd realized for himself that no one was *above* love.

The expression on Nick's face as he looked at her, his pale eyes warm with affection, unnerved her. What had happened to him in the few days since she'd seen him last, rolling in poison ivy in the woods behind the park? While she hadn't broken out, she could see that he had. He'd pushed up the sleeves of his jersey, where the healing rash had dried on his forearms. He wore an old hockey jersey with faded jeans, tight and worn at the seams. His feet, long and narrow, were bare, sinking into the plush beige carpet like the heels of her sandals.

She drew in a breath and struggled to focus on anything but him. Across the street from the tall windows of his condo, the Grand River rippled and glistened with afternoon sunshine. Nick had a great view and his condo development, in a renovated furniture factory, was just around the corner from the hospital. No wonder he'd balked at leaving Grand Rapids.

"Josh didn't tell me you were moving to Cloverville." Not that she'd given him much of a chance. After she'd left Nick's father in the park, she'd been so furious that Josh hadn't managed much more than a single word before handing her Nick's key. Too bad she'd had to work, but Clayton, sensing her dangerous mood, had let her go early.

"Why are you mad at me?" he asked again.

She struggled to remember. Those pale green eyes stared at her, bright with emotion, and she lost track of her thoughts, of time itself. Then she remembered. "You fixed the colonel."

"Dad worked on it, not me. Did he finish it?" He returned his attention to the box in which he'd been packing stereo components, ignoring her as he had all those years she'd volunteered at the hospital.

Her impatience surged back, and she kicked the box away from him.

Instead of responding with anger, the corners of his mouth lifted in an amused grin. "You're that mad that I had Dad fix the colonel?"

"No." Frustration frayed her nerves. But along with the

frustration there was strength. Not only had she finally realized how strong she was, she'd tapped into that strength to fight for what she wanted.

Nick shook his head as if confused, but his eyes gleamed. "Then, I don't understand."

"I'm the one who doesn't understand. Why didn't you tell me about your mom? About where you grew up. How you grew up." Tears burned her eyes, and she blinked furiously. "No, you don't have to answer that. I know you didn't want to let me into your life. You didn't want me to get any closer."

"That's right."

He didn't lie to her. She should appreciate that, but it deflated her anger, left her defeated. And hurt. And mad at herself now, for being stupid, for ignoring all those warnings— even her own—and falling for him anyway.

"I told you about my brother, though," he reminded her. "And that's the toughest thing I've ever had to deal with. I didn't even know my mom. I can't remember her. It wasn't like what you went through when you lost your dad. I was just a baby when she died."

"How did she die?"

"A car accident."

She nodded, understanding even more his reasons for becoming a doctor.

"Like I said, I don't remember her. I don't remember the crash, but my dad told me when I got old enough and started bugging him with questions." He swallowed hard, as if struggling with emotion. "Bruce and I were in the car with her. Even though Bruce's leg was broken, he got himself out and came back for me. The car had rolled over, but it was still running and leaking gas. Dangerous as hell, but he got me out and to safety. He couldn't get to her in time, and he probably wouldn't have been able to help her if he had. He'd been just a kid himself—only ten."

She let the tears fall now, burning streaks down her face. No wonder Bruce had been his hero—he'd saved his life. And for years Nick had wished he'd been able to return the favor. Her heart ached for him. "I'm sorry. I know how much it hurts to lose a parent."

"I don't," he said, as if dismissing her concern, her sympathy. "I never knew her. You can't miss what you've never known."

Yet his voice held a wistful quality. He might not have known her personally, but Colleen was certain his father had talked about Evelyn so much that Nick regretted never having had a chance to know her.

His mouth lifted in a slight grin, the dimple a shallow indentation in his cheek. "And my dad is still around. He's something else. Well, you met him."

"He's a sweetheart." On her way out of town, she'd spied him in Mrs. Hild's yard, admiring her flowers. The older woman's face had been flushed pink, and Colleen suspected it wasn't because of physical exertion in the yard. She'd been a widow for far too long to know how to handle a man's attention. "He's very charming."

His grin widened. "Now you know where I get it."

"Get what?" she teased, then giggled as he reached for her. His arms slid around her waist, but instead of pulling her close for a kiss, his fingers traveled up and down her ribs, tickling her until she squirmed free and dodged away from him.

"So are you done being mad yet?" he asked.

"No," she said, even though she could summon no more anger, not after what he'd told her. "I'm not through with you."

"I hope not," he murmured, his expression serious as he stared at her.

She drew in a shaky breath, forcing herself to remember all her reasons for seeking him out. Like his father had said, he needed to explain himself to her. But more than that, Colleen needed to explain herself to him. "You're not going to stop me from volunteering at the hospital."

He pushed his hand through his hair, tousling the golden strands. "I never meant to."

"You know you left me no choice," she pointed out. "If I showed up at the hospital, you'd think I was chasing you, trying to land a doctor."

"I'm sorry I ever suggested that," he said. "I know you're not."

"Then you'd be wrong again," she told him. "I do want a doctor."

His eyebrows rose above his pale eyes as surprise flashed across his face. "Colleen?"

"I want *you*."

Chapter Sixteen

Colleen held her breath as she watched his face for any reaction to her admission. His jaw clenched, a muscle ticking in his cheek. Her skin heating with embarrassment, she backed toward the door, wanting to leave before she made an even bigger fool of herself.

But Nick followed, kicking aside a pile of boxes in order to close his hands over her shoulders and pull her to him.

"Nick?" she asked, her heart beating madly as she stared at his unreadable face.

"I want you, Colleen. How I want you!"

Want. Not *love.*

He swept her up in his arms, kicking more cartons aside as he carried her toward a bedroom. He hadn't started packing there yet. No boxes littered the floor, so he moved quickly toward the bed and deposited her on the tangled sheets. When he followed her down, Colleen lifted her hands and pressed them against his chest, holding him back. "Want?"

"What?"

"You just *want* me? That's all?" She had been a fool to think anything had changed, to think that *he* had changed just because *she* had.

"I let that be enough in the park, and I shouldn't have." Not that she regretted making love with him. She'd never known such pleasure. "I deserve more than desire."

"Colleen…"

"I deserve love!" Her fire returned, coursing through her veins, so that she trembled with it. "For so many years, you didn't even notice me.

"It's not your fault," she said, absolving him. "No one noticed me. I think I wanted it that way, so I made sure no one noticed or heard me." She'd been like a hurt animal, hiding her pain and her vulnerability. "But I'm going to let my light shine now day and night," she informed him.

"It always did."

"I'm sick of being invisible," she continued her rant, unwilling to let him interrupt or distract her. "I'm sick of worrying about what everyone else wants or needs. For the first time in eight years, I'm going to be selfish."

"You said you only *wanted* me," he reminded her, amusement lightening his voice.

She slammed her hand against his chest. "Because I love you!"

"Hitting me is probably not the best way to prove that," he teased, catching and holding her hand, palm flat, against his hammering heart. "You told me that you didn't love me. That day in the park, you assured me that I didn't have to worry— that you hadn't fallen for me."

Her face heated with embarrassment again, and she dropped her gaze from his to the line of his jaw, to which golden stubble clung. He must have been so focused on packing that he hadn't bothered shaving.

His finger slid under her chin, tipping it up. "Colleen?"

"I lied to you," she admitted. She blew out a shaky breath.

"Don't feel bad. I lied to myself, too. I thought that I didn't love you that much yet. That it wouldn't hurt me if I lost you then. But if I lost you later…"

"It might destroy you?" he asked.

She should have known that he, of all people, would understand her fear. He'd watched how his older brother's marriage breaking up had destroyed his idol, his hero.

"Like losing my father had destroyed my mother," she explained.

"I met your mother at the wedding," he reminded her. "And the next morning, when she told me I could find you in the park. She seems fine now."

"She is," Colleen verified. "She recovered. But I didn't think I was as strong as my mother. I thought only strong people could survive loving and losing."

He sighed. "And I thought that because of Bruce not *even* strong people could survive losing. So it was better not to love anyone. Ever."

"I believed that, too," she admitted. "I didn't intend to ever risk loving anyone, either. But I do. I love you." She trembled with fear, and not the fear of loving him. She'd realized, after he'd gone, that she was strong enough to deal with losing him. But she was afraid that he wouldn't let himself love her back. "And I want you to love me."

"I do," he said as solemnly as if he spoke vows.

Tears of relief, of joy, sprang to her eyes. "Nick…"

"I have loved you since the moment I first saw you—in the church. It was love at first sight."

His words dimmed her happiness. "But you saw me before that. That wasn't the—"

"It was the first time *I* saw you, Colleen. And I fell for you right there, before I even knew your name. It was kismet, destiny, something that when other people talked about it, I thought they were fools." His chest rumbled beneath her palms as he laughed.

She blinked back tears, in disbelief that he returned her feelings. "You really love me?"

"Why do you think I'm moving to *Cloverville?*" he asked. "I love you and I want to be close to you."

"I didn't know." And she hadn't dared to hope that he returned her feelings.

"I had my life all figured out," he said, his voice heavy with irony. "But you messed up everything."

"I messed up your life?"

Nick regretted saying that, along with all the other stupid things he'd said to her. "No. You *gave* me a life. And I want to share it with you. I was going to do this right and ask Clayton for your hand in marriage."

"Like Josh did?" she asked. "Maybe it's best we don't follow the same traditions he and Molly followed."

"You're right," he agreed. Ordinarily, he wouldn't be superstitious, but Colleen's happiness was too important to risk. He had hoped she'd been lying that day when she'd claimed she hadn't loved him. But even if she didn't love him yet, he'd intended to make her fall for him—as deeply as he'd fallen for her.

"Let's not get married in the church," he suggested, wincing as he remembered the open window in the bride's dressing room.

"Abby and Clayton already have it booked," she said. "For their wedding."

He grinned. "I guess she accepted his apology then."

"And his proposal. And my mother's old engagement ring. Dad gave it to Clayton before he died, to give to his bride. I think he'd hoped Clayton would give it to Abby someday and officially make her a McClintock."

He offered a proposal of his own, "Let's get married in the park."

"I haven't said yes yet," she pointed out. Her voice turning haughty like the first time she'd ever spoken to him, and she added, "In fact, you haven't even asked me the question yet."

A grin pulled at his lips. She made him so damned happy— happier than he'd ever thought a man could be. "I thought we weren't following tradition."

"You're right. Let me ask you." She squirmed out from beneath his body, rolled off the bed and knelt beside where he lay. "Will you marry me, Nick Jameson?"

"Yes, I will marry you, Colleen McClintock," he agreed, and pulled her up onto the bed with him and into his arms. "I wasn't wrong about everything. I knew that the longer I knew you, the more I would love you."

"That's why you left."

"But I couldn't stay away. I had to see you." He smoothed his fingers across her cheek. "I had to touch you." He leaned closer, pressing his mouth against hers, taking her lips in a deep, hungry kiss. "I had to kiss you."

Breathing hard, she reminded him, "You're forgetting one thing."

"This?" he asked as he undid the buttons on her blouse and pulled it from her shoulders, leaving her bare from the waist up but for a thin cotton bra.

She shook her head, locks of dark hair slipping free of the knot at the back of her neck. He had dreamed of her thick, dark hair spread across his pillows. He had dreamed of her in his bed.

He unhooked the metal thing at her waist. Then he slid his

palms over her narrow hips, pushing down the skirt. He cupped her buttocks, lifting her hips against his eager body. "This?"

She shook her head again.

"My clothes?" he asked. With reluctance, he lifted himself off her just long enough to toss his shirt aside and shuck his jeans and briefs. Skin slid over skin, limbs tangling, as he rejoined her. "Colleen…"

"No," she said even as she wrapped her arms around him and lifted her legs to cradle his hips. "You're forgetting that I was the one to come to you."

Even as passion consumed him, heating his skin and fraying his nerves so that he shook with need for her, he laughed. "You beat me this once."

"Twice," she insisted, her breath catching as he undid her bra and tore her panties aside, giving him access with his hands, with his lips. "I saw you first."

And she'd known that first time, no matter what the rumors about his lack of a heart, that he was the man for her. His fingers caressed her breasts, teasing her nipples as he moved his mouth across her belly, then lower, bringing her to a shattering release. She lay spent, her fingers knotted in his rumpled sheets.

"And I beat you again," she said, still catching her breath.

Laughter rumbled in his chest as he pulled her close, then thrust inside her. His teeth clenched together for self-control, he moved slowly, murmuring, "As long as I have you in my life, Colleen, I can't lose."

She lifted her hips, meeting each thrust, their bodies in perfect sync. She dug her nails into his shoulders, scraped them down his back to his buttocks. Pleasure crashed through her again, wave after wave. "Nick!"

With a guttural cry, he joined her. Then he rolled them, so

that she lay atop him, her body limp. His heart beat hard beneath her cheek. His hands, shaking slightly, ran down her back. "I love you."

"I love you, too. And I love being able to tell you that I do."

Instead of keeping it to herself—or from herself, as she had for so long.

"No more secrets?"

She shook her head. "No more secrets." She sighed, not wanting reality to intrude on their happiness. "That's not going to be a problem."

"But?" They were so attuned that he'd obviously heard the word in her voice.

"We have another problem."

His body tensed beneath hers. "What?"

"My sister. She means to me what Bruce meant to you. She's not just my sister. She's my friend. Are you ever going to be able to forgive her for leaving Josh at the altar?" She braced her palms against his chest, so she could lever up and see his eyes.

"She hurt Josh." He sighed. "Probably his pride more than his heart. I don't think he loves her."

"And I don't think she loves him," Colleen shared. "That's why she took off."

"Then why did she agree to marry him in the first place?" he asked, his voice rough with frustration.

"People, even people we love and admire, don't always make the wisest choices," she reminded him gently. "I really want you and Molly to get along, to become friends. You're so much alike. Molly decided to be a doctor when our dad died, for the same reasons you did."

"Because I wasn't able to save Bruce…"

"Or your mother. And you wanted to save other people."

Nick's heart expanded, swelling with love for her. No one, not even Josh, had ever understood him like she did. "For you, I'll forget about Molly leaving Josh at the altar. I'll be her friend." He tangled his fingers in her hair, pushing a lock behind her ear. "For you, I'm even moving to Cloverville."

She glanced around his bedroom, at the shuttered windows, the exposed brick and wood beams in the coffered ceiling. "I can't believe you'd give up this place. You haven't sold it yet?"

He shook his head. "I have an appointment with a Realtor, though."

"Cancel it," she advised him. "Let's keep it."

"You don't want to live in Cloverville?"

"I don't care where we are, as long as we're together," she said, settling her head back against his chest.

"But I already bought a house—which I probably shouldn't have done before asking you," he realized. "I acted like an arrogant ass again, huh? Making decisions that'll affect both of us."

"Your dad warned me," she said, her voice soft with affection. "That you're a handful. But don't worry, I can handle you."

She was younger and less experienced, but Nick had no doubt she could hold her own against him. She already held his heart. "Yes, you can." The way she'd slammed into his house tonight, and into his heart when he first noticed her, he had no doubt she could handle him very well.

"I might even come to work for you, if you ask me nicely," she said.

"At the office?" he asked, stunned that she'd offer. He knew how much family meant to her.

She nodded. "I can manage it. Clayton doesn't need me. I'd already thought about quitting the insurance office to work for Abby."

"She has a temporary employment agency?" he verified, remembering Clayton mentioning it as the man had been unable to talk about, to think about, anything but Abby Hamilton. Nick understood that kind of fascination with a woman. Would Clayton accept Nick as a suitable husband for his little sister? Nick might have to prove himself to the other man, to prove how much he loved Colleen and would never hurt her.

Colleen nodded. "But I'd rather work for you."

"*With* me," he corrected her, happiness splitting his face into a wide grin. He couldn't imagine anything he'd enjoy more than spending all his time with Colleen at his side.

"With you," she agreed with a happy sigh, her breath warming his skin.

He fought the distraction of her naked body pressed against his and reached for the drawer of the bedside table. Pulling out a small velvet box, he playfully mused, "Since we're skipping tradition, I don't suppose you'd be interested in this."

Colleen lifted her chin from his shoulder. "You bought me a ring?"

"I told you I planned on doing this right."

"Are we doing it wrong now?" she asked, brushing her hair against his chest as she moved over his body. She rubbed against him, reawakening his desire for her. He would never be able to get enough of her, no matter how much time, how many years or lifetimes, they were together.

"I don't think we could ever do it wrong," Nick maintained.

She reached for the box, but he pulled it back, teasing her. "Since we've decided not to follow tradition…"

She caught his wrist and pulled his hand toward her. "Show me the ring."

He flipped open the velvet lid, and she gasped. He glanced

toward the ring he'd chosen. "You don't like it. It's too big? Too gaudy? I should have had you pick it out."

He'd been so determined to live out his life as a single, he would have to work on how to behave as a couple. Colleen wouldn't be just his wife, she'd be his partner, his best friend. Somehow, he thought Josh would understand being re-placed—in fact, he'd probably be overjoyed.

Colleen held out her slightly trembling hand. "Try it on me."

He slid the platinum band onto her long, slender finger. "It fits perfectly. But the stone looks even bigger on your hand." But he'd wanted to do it right, to impress her so much that she wouldn't be able to turn down his proposal or his love, and so he'd picked out the biggest diamond in the store. A square-cut three-carat rock. "Everyone's going to notice that."

A smile of satisfaction spread across her face as she nodded. "I told you I'm through with being invisible." She whistled. "This'll help my light shine."

"So it'll do?" he asked.

"Yes."

"And me?"

Her smile widened as she turned her attention from the ring to him. She rubbed her breasts against his chest, then glided his erection inside her wet heat. A breath shuddered out of her parted lips as he lifted his hips, moving deep inside her. "You'll do."

Epilogue

"We're supposed to carry the rings," TJ argued with the best man, his father, as Josh slid the wedding band into his pocket.

"Colleen will kill us if we lose her ring," Nick said, staving off the twins' argument.

TJ gave a solemn nod. Buzz could barely move after their last turn on the merry-go-round. He lagged behind as they walked toward where the minister stood next to the properly mended statue of Colonel Clover. Thanks to Nick's dad's expertise, the colonel looked better than he probably originally had.

"Colleen does know how to slay dragons," TJ said, his blue eyes wide with awe.

Nick remembered the book she'd read them in this very park, the one about the princess who'd slayed her own dragons. Like Colleen had. She felt no more guilt over her youthful mistake. No more fear over risking her heart. She was so strong, and Nick couldn't be prouder or more impatient to make her his wife.

Loving her had made him strong, too—strong enough to forgive himself his past and to risk his future and his heart with her. But loving Colleen wasn't a risk. It was the smartest thing he'd ever done. He waved at the boys as his dad took their hands and led them toward the tent behind the chairs, where his bride and the rest of the wedding party were getting ready to walk down the aisle. He had no fear of Colleen leaving him at the altar; he had no doubt that she loved him as much as he loved her.

Endlessly.

Moments later, Mrs. Hild began the wedding march on the organ borrowed from the church. Colleen tightened her grasp on her older brother's arm as he led her across the grass, following the trail of white rose petals her flower girl, Lara McClintock, had dropped as she'd walked down the aisle between Buzz and TJ. Clayton had adopted Abby's daughter, making her his own in every way that mattered. Colleen blinked back tears over her brother's complete happiness. Her mother and Molly had been right to meddle. Clayton and Abby and Lara belonged together. Forever.

Just like Colleen and Nick.

Clayton escorted her to where her groom waited for her, in the shadow of Colonel Clover, who presided proudly over the park and her wedding. "Nervous?" her older brother asked, his voice a whisper.

She should have been, as everyone had risen from their chairs to turn and stare at her. But she lifted her chin, taking their interest as a compliment. She knew she looked beautiful today. Her bridesmaids had seen to it, weaving red carnations and white lilies into her hair. She hadn't had the heart to tell them how quickly Nick would mess up their handiwork.

Just like she'd messed up his life—for the better. She'd never seen him so happy, his handsome face creased with a wide grin, the lone dimple denting his cheek, as she and Clayton approached.

Her brother lifted her veil and kissed her cheek before

shaking Nick's hand. But he didn't immediately take his seat beside their mother and her new husband, Wallace Schipper. Instead, he patted the protruding belly of the matron of honor, his wife, Abby, who would soon have their child. Beside her stood Colleen's other attendants. Brenna and Molly, looking gorgeous in matching sundresses, the same shade of blue as the cloudless sky.

Abby smiled, her face aglow with happiness, as she took the bride's bouquet. Then Colleen turned toward her groom. Nick clasped her hands in his, holding them tight as if he wanted to make sure she never ran away from him.

"I love you," she assured him. "I'm going to love you forever. I think I already have."

"And I love you, Colleen," he vowed. "You're my heart, my life, my whole world."

While she knew that would have scared him before, now she saw no fear in his gleaming eyes—only love. Endless love.

* * * * *

*Something's going on between Josh and Brenna—
find out their secret in the next book in*
THE WEDDING PARTY *miniseries,*
FOREVER HIS BRIDE,
coming August 2008,
only from Harlequin American Romance.

THOROUGHBRED LEGACY
The stakes are high when it comes to love,
horse racing, family secrets
and broken promises.

A new exciting
Harlequin continuity series
coming soon!
Led by New York Times *bestselling author*
Elizabeth Bevarly
FLIRTING WITH TROUBLE

Here's a preview!

THE DOOR CLOSED behind them, throwing them into darkness and leaving them utterly alone. And the next thing Daniel knew, he heard himself saying, "Marnie, I'm sorry about the way things turned out in Del Mar."

She said nothing at first, only strode across the room and stared out the window beside him. Although he couldn't see her well in the darkness—he still hadn't switched on a light... but then, neither had she—he imagined her expression was a little preoccupied, a little anxious, a little confused.

Finally, very softly, she said, "Are you?"

He nodded, then, worried she wouldn't be able to see the gesture, added, "Yeah. I am. I should have said goodbye to you."

"Yes, you should have."

Actually, he thought, there were a lot of things he should have done in Del Mar. He'd had *a lot* riding on the Pacific Classic, and even more on his entry, Little Joe, but after meeting Marnie, the Pacific Classic had been the last thing on Daniel's mind. His loss at Del Mar had pretty much ended his career before it had even begun, and he'd had to start all over again, rebuilding from nothing.

He simply had not then and did not now have room in his

life for a woman as potent as Marnie Roberts. He was a horseman first and foremost. From the time he was a schoolboy, he'd known what he wanted to do with his life—be the best possible trainer he could be.

He had to make sure Marnie understood—and he understood, too—why things had ended the way they had eight years ago. He just wished he could find the words to do that. Hell, he wished he could find the *thoughts* to do that.

"You made me forget things, Marnie, things that I really needed to remember. And that scared the hell out of me. Little Joe should have won the Classic. He was by far the best horse entered in that race. But I didn't give him the attention he needed and deserved that week, because all I could think about was you. Hell, when I woke up that morning all I wanted to do was lie there and look at you, and then wake you up and make love to you again. If I hadn't left when I did— the way I did—I might still be lying there in that bed with you, thinking about nothing else."

"And would that be so terrible?" she asked.

"Of course not," he told her. "But that wasn't why I was in Del Mar," he repeated. "I was in Del Mar to win a race. That was my job. And my work was the most important thing to me."

She said nothing for a moment, only studied his face in the darkness as if looking for the answer to a very important question. Finally she asked, "And what's the most important thing to you now, Daniel?"

Wasn't the answer to that obvious? "My work," he answered automatically.

She nodded slowly. "Of course," she said softly. "That is, after all, what you do best."

Her comment, too, puzzled him. She made it sound as if being good at what he did was a bad thing.

She bit her lip thoughtfully, her eyes fixed on his, glimmering in the scant moonlight that was filtering through the window. And damned if Daniel didn't find himself wanting to pull her into his arms and kiss her. But as much as it might have felt as if no time had passed since Del Mar, there were eight years between now and then. And eight years was a long time in the best of circumstances. For Daniel and Marnie, it was virtually a lifetime.

So Daniel turned and started for the door, then halted. He couldn't just walk away and leave things as they were, unsettled. He'd done that eight years ago and regretted it.

"It *was* good to see you again, Marnie," he said softly. And since he was being honest, he added, "I hope we see each other again."

She didn't say anything in response, only stood silhouetted against the window with her arms wrapped around her in a way that made him wonder whether she was doing it because she was cold, or if she just needed something—someone—to hold on to. In either case, Daniel understood. There was an emptiness clinging to him that he suspected would be there for a long time.

* * * * *

THOROUGHBRED LEGACY
coming soon wherever books are sold!

Thoroughbred *Legacy*

Launching in June 2008

A dramatic new 12-book continuity that embodies the American Dream.

Meet the Prestons, owners of Quest Stables, a successful horse-racing and breeding empire. But the lives, loves and reputations of this hardworking family are put at risk when a breeding scandal unfolds.

Flirting with Trouble

by *New York Times* bestselling author

ELIZABETH BEVARLY

Eight years ago, publicist Marnie Roberts spent seven days of bliss with Australian horse trainer Daniel Whittleson. But just as quickly, he disappeared. Now Marnie is heading to Australia to finally confront the man she's never been able to forget.

The stakes are high when it comes to love, horse racing, family secrets and broken promises.

A new exciting Harlequin continuity series coming soon!

Cole's Red-Hot Pursuit

Cole Westmoreland is a man who gets what he
wants. And he wants independent and sultry
Patrina Forman! She resists him—until a Montana
blizzard traps them together. For three delicious
nights, Cole indulges Patrina with his brand of
seduction. When the sun comes out, Cole and
Patrina are left to wonder—will this be the end of
the passion that storms between them?

Look for

COLE'S RED-HOT
PURSUIT

by USA TODAY bestselling author

BRENDA
JACKSON

Available in June 2008 wherever you buy books.

Always Powerful, Passionate and Provocative.

REQUEST YOUR FREE BOOKS!

2 FREE NOVELS PLUS 2
FREE GIFTS!

Heart, Home & Happiness!

YES! Please send me 2 FREE Harlequin American Romance® novels and my 2 FREE gifts (gifts are worth about $10). After receiving them, if I don't wish to receive any more books, I can return the shipping statement marked "cancel." If I don't cancel, I will receive 4 brand-new novels every month and be billed just $4.24 per book in the U.S. or $4.99 per book in Canada, plus 25¢ shipping and handling per book and applicable taxes, if any*. That's a savings of close to 15% off the cover price! I understand that accepting the 2 free books and gifts places me under no obligation to buy anything. I can always return a shipment and cancel at any time. Even if I never buy another book from Harlequin, the two free books and gifts are mine to keep forever.

154 HDN EEZK   354 HDN EEZV

Name _____ (PLEASE PRINT) _____

Address _____ Apt. # _____

City _____ State/Prov. _____ Zip/Postal Code _____

Signature (if under 18, a parent or guardian must sign)

Mail to the **Harlequin Reader Service:**
IN U.S.A.: P.O. Box 1867, Buffalo, NY 14240-1867
IN CANADA: P.O. Box 609, Fort Erie, Ontario L2A 5X3

Not valid to current subscribers of Harlequin American Romance books.

Want to try two free books from another line?
Call 1-800-873-8635 or visit www.morefreebooks.com.

* Terms and prices subject to change without notice. N.Y. residents add applicable sales tax. Canadian residents will be charged applicable provincial taxes and GST. This offer is limited to one order per household. All orders subject to approval. Credit or debit balances in a customer's account(s) may be offset by any other outstanding balance owed by or to the customer. Please allow 4 to 6 weeks for delivery. Offer available while quantities last.

Your Privacy: Harlequin is committed to protecting your privacy. Our Privacy Policy is available online at www.eHarlequin.com or upon request from the Reader Service. From time to time we make our lists of customers available to reputable third parties who may have a product or service of interest to you. If you would prefer we not share your name and address, please check here. ☐

HAR08

Inside ROMANCE

Stay up-to-date on all your
romance reading news!

Inside Romance is a FREE quarterly newsletter
highlighting our upcoming series releases
and promotions.

Visit
www.eHarlequin.com/InsideRomance
to sign up to receive our complimentary newsletter today!

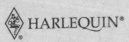